FALLING FOR
MR MYSTERIOUS

FALLING FOR
MR MYSTERIOUS

BY

BARBARA HANNAY

MILLS
BOON

First published in Great Britain 2012
by Mills & Boon, an imprint of Harlequin (UK) Limited.
Large Print edition 2012
Harlequin (UK) Limited, Eton House,
18-24 Paradise Road, Richmond, Surrey TW9 1SR

© Barbara Hannay 2012

ISBN: 978 0 263 22612 6

Harlequin (UK) policy is to use papers that are natural,
renewable and recyclable products and made from
wood grown in sustainable forests. The logging and
manufacturing process conform to the legal environmental
regulations of the country of origin.

Printed and bound in Great Britain
by CPI Antony Rowe, Chippenham, Wiltshire

CHAPTER ONE

WHEN the train drew in to Roma Street Station, Emily checked her phone messages one more time. There was still nothing from Alex, so now she was officially worried—not only about Alex's twenty-four-hour silence, but also about her own fate. She had no idea what she'd do if he wasn't in Brisbane.

She'd rushed to the city in blind despair. She needed to see Alex, to stay with him and, yes, to pour out her heart to him. Of all her family, Alex would understand, and Emily had been so very desperate to get away from Wandabilla that she'd jumped on the train in the vain hope that Alex would return her call before she arrived.

Now, the train came to a stop with a wheezing sigh of brakes and, all around Emily, passengers were rising from their seats, gathering their belongings in a businesslike fashion, pulling on jackets and coats and heading for the carriage doors, eager to be out on the platform and gone.

They, of course, had somewhere to go.

Emily did not.

If Alex was away, she would have to find a hotel. She certainly wasn't going to turn tail and head home to Wandabilla, to face the music, with everyone in the small country town knowing what had happened to her.

Besides, Emily told herself, there was still a slim chance that Alex was home. He might have a problem with his phone, or perhaps he'd let the battery run down, or he'd bought a new phone and changed his number and hadn't got around to telling her.

Although her doubts about the wisdom of rushing to Brisbane were mounting fast, she rolled the magazine she'd been trying unsuccessfully to read and stowed it in her shoulder bag, then retrieved her suitcase from the luggage rack.

It was an unusually cold August afternoon, and a biting westerly wind whistled callously along the platform. Shivering, Emily buttoned her coat and turned up its collar, then she lugged her suitcase behind her and headed for the warmth of the pedestrian tunnel.

As luck would have it, she was in the depths of the tunnel, jostling with crowds of shoppers and commuters, when she heard the soft *quack-quack*, which was the silly ringtone she used to distinguish social from business calls. She grabbed her phone from her bag. It was a text message.

Em, sorry I missed you, and very sorry to hear about that @#$%$# of a boyfriend. Wish I could be with you now, but I'm in Frankfurt at a Book Fair. Please use the apartment tho. Stay as long as you like and use my room. I've checked with Jude and he's cool, so he's expecting you.
Hugs,
Alex xxx

Emily had to read this twice, standing rock still in the tunnel while commuters steered somewhat irritably around her. She needed a moment to take the message in, to deal with her see-sawing emotions of relief that Alex was OK, and her disappointment that he was so far away.

Very quickly, overriding these initial reactions, rushed a flurry of questions. Who was this Jude person? When had he arrived in Alex's life? And…would he really be as cool as her cousin suggested about her sudden appearance on his doorstep?

She felt awkward about imposing on a stranger and she wondered, briefly, if she should continue up the coast to her grandmother's instead. Granny Silver was as understanding and welcoming as Alex, but she preferred to see the world through rose-coloured glasses, so Emily rarely burdened her with her problems.

Also, if this Jude fellow was expecting her, and if he was anything like Alex—which he probably was, remembering Alex's former housemates—he'd probably already jumped into host mode.

Jude could well be whipping up something delicious for their dinner right now, so it would be rude to simply not turn up. Emily headed to a nearby bottle shop, bought a good quality red as well as a white, because she didn't know Jude's tastes, then went to the taxi rank. But as the taxi sped towards West End, crossing a bridge over the wide Brisbane River, her impulsive dash to the city began to feel more foolish than ever.

She'd been so self-absorbed, so totally desperate to get away from prying eyes, that she'd seen her cousin Alex as her one safe haven. She'd had visions of crying on his shoulder, of sitting with him on his balcony, looking out over the river and the city skyline, drinking wine together while she told him all about the whole sorry mess with Michael.

Alex was such a wonderful listener, way better than her mum. He never trotted out *I told you so*, or kindly but firmly pointed out her mistakes. Best of all, once he'd sympathised and mopped her tears, he always made her laugh.

Man, she could do with a laugh right now, but she couldn't expect sympathy, wine and cheering up from Alex's new flatmate. As the taxi drew up outside the apartment block, she told herself that the best she could hope for was friendly tolerance from this perfect stranger, and a little privacy in which to nurse her wounded feelings.

At any rate, it was reassuring to know that she

wouldn't have to negotiate any of the bothersome boy-meets-girl nonsense. She'd had enough trouble with men to last her a lifetime, but she could rely on the fact that any man living with Alex would be gay and totally safe to live with.

Jude Marlowe was still typing at his laptop when the doorbell rang. He was in the midst of a thought, a decent thought, one of the few he'd come up with that day. He was trying to get it onto the page so he continued typing, despite the doorbell, knowing that if he stopped, the precious words would be lost, never to be recalled.

The bell rang again, with a slight air of desperation. Fortunately, the last sentence was captured and Jude saved his work and pushed away from the desk. Taking off his reading glasses, he rubbed at the bridge of his nose, then stood unhurriedly and stretched, rolling his shoulders in a bid to ease the tension that always locked in when he became too absorbed in his writing.

The caller would be Alex's young cousin. Jude had received a garbled message that she needed a bed for a few nights and so he'd manfully hidden his reluctance to socialise and assured Alex that he'd oblige. Apparently, she'd had boyfriend trouble and was suffering from a broken heart.

Another of Alex's lame ducks, Jude thought wryly, knowing he was one, too.

He was in the hallway, blinking at the darkness—was it really that late?—before he gave a thought to his appearance. Still in the clothes he'd dragged on in the morning, he was wearing old, badly ripped jeans and a baggy, ancient football jersey, stained at the neck and worn at the elbows. Not exactly suitable for receiving Alex's houseguest, but it was too late to do anything about it. The girl at the door would be getting impatient.

Jude turned on the light as he pulled the door open and a yellow glow spilled, golden and honey-warm, over the chilled figure outside. At first sight of her, he felt deprived of oxygen.

Later, he asked himself what he'd been expecting, and he realised that if he'd given Alex's lovelorn country cousin any thought at all, he'd mentally classified her as frumpy and miserable. An unfashionable, possibly plain, country mouse.

How wrong he was.

The girl standing before Jude in a stylish white wool coat and knee-high brown leather boots was a stunner. Her red-gold hair flowed softly over her white lapels, making him think of fire on snow. Her face was delicate yet full of character.

And while there was a hint of sadness about her blue eyes, her skin showed no sign of country mouse freckles. Her complexion was fair and smooth, her chin neat, her mouth curving and smiley.

She looked, at first glance, like all Jude's female fantasies rolled into one hot package.

He found himself silenced to the point of stupidity.

'You must be Jude?' she enquired, tilting her head to one side and smiling cautiously.

'Sure.' Somehow, he remembered his manners. 'And you must be Emily.'

'Yes. Emily Silver, Alex's cousin.' She held out her hand. 'How do you do, Jude? Alex said he'd warned you about me.'

'Yes, he rang.' But the warning had been totally inadequate, Jude realised now. He'd planned to offer the barest courtesies as a host and then leave Emily Silver to mend her heart in whichever way she needed to. He still planned to do that, but already he knew she wouldn't be easy to ignore.

'I must say it's very kind of you to take me in at such short notice.' She shook his hand, and it was a ridiculously electrifying experience.

'You're very welcome.' Jude spoke gruffly to cover his dazed dismay. Then he noticed her suitcase. 'I'll get that for you.'

'Oh, thanks. And I've brought wine.' With a dazzling smile, she held up a brown paper bag. 'A bottle of each.'

There was a slight shuffle in the doorway as he stepped forward to reach for the luggage while Emily came inside. Their bodies brushed briefly. *Damn.* Jude couldn't believe he was reacting this way. He'd had more than his fair share of girlfriends, but this evening his body was reacting as if he'd been cast away on a desert island and Emily was the first woman he'd seen in two decades.

'Oh, it's lovely and warm inside,' she was saying.

Jude nodded, adding grouchily, 'Alex's room is

down the hall, as I'm sure you remember. First on the left.'

In the doorway to the master bedroom, Emily paused and sent a dimpling smile back to him over her shoulder. 'Wow. I've never stayed in this room. I'll be able to enjoy the amazing view of the river from Alex's bed.'

'No doubt.' Jude set the suitcase on the floor just inside the doorway, angry that the mere mention of the word *bed* set his mind diving into fantasy land. Refusing to meet her animated gaze, he said tersely, 'You settle in. I'll…ah… be in the kitchen.'

In the kitchen, he stared disconsolately at the contents of the refrigerator while he rated himself as several versions of a fool. It made absolutely no sense that he'd been sideswiped by Alex's country cousin.

Sure, she was a looker. But her beauty was irrelevant in this situation. She'd come to the city to escape from a low-lying jerk of a boyfriend, while Jude had problems of his own. He was in the city for medical tests that freaked the hell out of him.

And yet, when he'd seen Emily on the doorstep, there'd been an out-of-this-world moment when he'd forgotten all of this. Now, he'd plummeted back to earth. And to common sense.

Emily was sharing this apartment, and yes, he'd promised Alex that he would keep an eye on her. But that could be covered by token exchanges. A few courteous words. Now and again. Nothing more than the most superficial hospitality was required.

He was grateful to have that sorted. He need show no more than cursory interest in this guest, which was just as well, considering everything that lay ahead of him.

Emily wondered if she'd made a terrible mistake as she sank onto the edge of Alex's king-size bed.

She was imposing on Alex's flatmate, and she could tell from the moment she'd first seen Jude that he wasn't thrilled about her sudden arrival. Now cold hopelessness washed over her as she saw her flight to Brisbane as just another mistake among the many mistakes she'd made lately.

She would have to reassure Jude that she wouldn't stay. Problem was, she wasn't ready to go back to Wandabilla, either. So, in the morning, she would have to check out accommodation options.

In the meantime…she would try to be as little trouble as possible for Jude.

He was very different from Alex. She'd seen this immediately. Physically, the two men were poles apart. Her cousin shared her auburn colouring and he was slim and scholarly-looking, while Jude was tall and dark, with the broad-shouldered, lean-hipped build of a man of action. Not too rugged or too chiselled, his looks were nicely in between.

But, of course, Alex always had good taste in men.

After taking off her coat, but not bothering to unpack, Emily went through to the kitchen and discovered another difference from Alex. Jude was no cook.

There was absolutely no action at the stove. In fact, Jude was standing in the middle of the kitchen, staring at the open pantry cupboard and scratching his head.

When he saw her, he gave an offhand shrug.

'I'm afraid I never think much about food when I'm caught up with my work.'

'Please, don't worry about feeding me,' she assured him. 'I'm happy to look after myself.' The last thing she wanted was to be any bother, but curiosity prompted her to ask, 'What sort of work do you do?'

Jude frowned, then spoke with obvious reluctance. 'I'm a writer, so I work from home, but I'm totally disorganized when it comes to meals. Sometimes I heat up a tin of soup for my dinner, but since I've been here in West End, I've mostly eaten takeaway.'

Emily guessed he was missing Alex's gourmet cooking. 'Honestly, I'm happy with takeaway,' she insisted. 'I know there's a host of great restaurants here. I could pop out now, if you like, and get something for both of us.'

She smiled, hoping to show Alex's flatmate that she really wanted to fit in as smoothly as possible. But smiling didn't seem to work with this man. His gaze darted away.

'I'll come with you,' he said.

'Are you sure?'

'I promised Alex I'd look after you.'

She almost told him not to bother. She was perfectly capable of walking a block or two to the shops, but she didn't want to start off on a bad footing. 'OK. I'll grab my coat and a scarf.'

They met again in the hallway, and Emily saw that Jude had changed lightning-fast into less tattered jeans as well as outdoor boots and a thick black woollen sweater.

Gosh—he was actually rather good-looking. Lucky Alex. Under other circumstances—circumstances in which she wasn't totally 'over men' and Jude Marlowe wasn't gay and standoffish—she might have taken second or third looks at him. And more, right now, she would have been far happier if he'd been less attractive, but empathetic and warm, like Alex.

Clearly this wasn't the case, and she would have to nurse her sorrows on her own. At any rate, she was relieved to be in the company of a man she could trust not to make a move on her.

Outside on the footpath, the wind made their cheeks pink, but Emily was snug in her coat and the air was invigorating—a beautiful clear and crisp winter's night in the city.

She was starting to feel a tiny bit better already. Of course, there was still a sickening ache in her chest whenever she thought about her former boyfriend, Michael, and a stomach-churning twist of appalling guilt whenever she thought about the wife and children he'd conveniently forgotten to mention. But just getting away from Wandabilla had helped. At least no one knew her here in Brisbane and she didn't have to face the gossip and curious glances.

The restaurants were filled with diners, talking and laughing and generally having a good time, and as Emily passed each doorway, she caught snatches of music and chatter and sensational appetising smells.

She came to a stop outside an Indian takeaway.

'Is this what you fancy?' Jude asked.

'I would love a curry. We only have Chinese in Wandabilla, and I adore Indian.'

'Indian it is then,' he said, stepping inside. 'Too easy.'

'Are you going out of your way to oblige me, or are you always this easy about meals?'

Jude's eyes shimmered. 'When it comes to food, I'm a pushover.'

They ordered two kinds of curries—one meat

and one vegetarian, as well as steamed rice and naan bread.

'And samosas,' said Jude. 'For entrée.'

Heading back to the apartment with their mouth-watering packages, he suddenly took a left-hand dive into a supermarket and emerged moments later with an armful of bright yellow daffodils.

'Wow—' Emily swallowed her surprise as he handed the sunshiny blooms to her '—what are these for?'

'I've heard you need cheering up.'

'Oh.' It was the lovely sort of thing Alex would have done. Perhaps Alex had given his house-mate instructions.

'That's so sweet,' she told him, feeling sud-denly, unexpectedly grateful, and just a tiny bit weepy. Impulsively, she stood on tiptoe and gave Jude a kiss on the cheek. To her surprise, a dark tide of colour stained his neck.

Afraid that she'd embarrassed him, she quickly changed the subject. 'Should we get something for breakfast while we're out?'

'Of course. Sorry. I've been a bit distracted lately.'

For the briefest moment, Emily saw something else in Jude's grey eyes—just a flash of a darker emotion that might have been anxiety or fear. It was gone almost as soon as it arrived, but it made her wonder if he'd been distracted by more than his work.

She couldn't exactly quiz him about it, so she turned her attention to their shopping, choosing food she thought a guy might like—eggs and bacon, and then a punnet of blueberries, a tub of yoghurt and a bag of good quality coffee. At the cash register, Jude insisted on paying, warding off her protests with a grim fierceness that was hard to fight.

A slight awkwardness descended as they hurried back to the apartment, laden with their purchases.

In the kitchen, Jude set the takeaway tubs on the table, then found cutlery and plates.

'Where do you normally eat?' Emily asked, not at all surprised when he frowned again. She'd already decided that his thoughtful purchase of flowers had been an aberration, and from now on she should probably expect frowns and grimness.

She half expected Jude to tell her that he preferred to eat on his own, hidden away in his
room in front of his computer.

But he said, 'Here's OK, isn't it?'

'Of course.' Emily tried not to look too surprised or pleased, but she couldn't deny that she
would prefer his company to being left alone
with her own unhappy thoughts. She shot him
a cautious smile. 'What about wine? Would you
rather red or white?'

'Actually…I'm not drinking alcohol.'

'Oh?'

'I've given it up. Temporarily.'

Once again, she thought she caught a flash
of emotion, as if there was something else, a
deeper worry that haunted Jude. For a second
she thought he was going to say more but, if that
was his plan, he quickly changed his mind.

'I won't have wine, either, then,' she said. 'It's
not a great idea to drink alone.'

'But you're not alone.' Jude was insistent. 'Go
on. Have a glass. It'll do you good. You want to
drown your sorrows, don't you?'

If only she could just drown her sorrows and
be rid of them. But the pain would still be there

when the effects of the wine wore off. Just the
same, as Jude peeled silver foil from the wonderfully aromatic tubs of curry, Emily poured
herself a glass of white and gratefully flopped
down in a seat.

'That smells amazing. I didn't eat lunch.'

'Neither did I. I'm starving.'

At first they were both too ravenous to bother
with conversation, but there were plenty of ap-
preciative groans and nods of approval as they
helped themselves to the food. Emily, however,
hadn't been able to eat much since she'd found
out about Michael, and it wasn't long before she
had to call a halt.

'My eyes were bigger than my stomach,' she
said as she watched Jude help himself to more
curry. She sipped her wine instead, then because
he was starting to look more relaxed, she gave in
to her growing curiosity. 'I hope you don't mind
my asking, but how long have you known Alex?'

He looked surprised. 'Why would I mind? I've
known him for about five years. As I said earlier, I'm a writer. Alex is my agent.'

'Oh? Really?' So they had a business relationship as well as a personal one. 'That's a handy arrangement.'

Jude frowned at her, as if, yet again, he found her comment puzzling. 'Yes, it is. Very handy.'

'What do you write?'

'Thrillers.'

She gaped at him. 'As in thriller novels?'

'Afraid so.'

'How amazing.' Now it was her turn to be surprised, and she stared at her mysterious host with new respect. 'Should I have heard of you?'

'Not unless you like reading thrillers.'

Emily liked reading crime novels, and she didn't mind a thriller plot, but she mostly read books written by women writers because they had more female characters in their stories. 'I'm not keen on the really blokesy books,' she said.

Jude actually smiled at that. 'To be honest, neither am I. In fact, I always include at least one major female character in every story.'

'Well—' her respect for him was growing by the second '—I should be reading your books then, shouldn't I?'

His head dipped in a mock bow.

Before Emily could ask anything else, he held up a hand as if to stop her. 'I think that's enough questions about me.'

'Ah...' Emily pulled a face. 'So now we talk about Alex? Or world affairs?'

'Or you.'

'Believe me,' she warned him darkly, 'you don't want to go there.'

While she'd come rushing to the city to tell Alex *everything* about Michael, she couldn't imagine ever confessing her personal problems to Jude. The very thought of telling him about her cheating boyfriend made her face burn. She took a swift and, hopefully, cooling gulp of wine.

As if he'd sensed her sudden panic, he said, 'I was wondering what sort of work you do.'

This, at least, was easy to answer. 'I work in a bank.'

'As a teller?'

'As a manager.'

'I beg your pardon?' His intelligent grey eyes narrowed. 'Do you mean you're a *bank* manager?'

'I do.'

Jude blinked at her.

'Don't you believe me?'

His smile was sheepish. 'I'm very sorry if I looked surprised, Emily. It's just—' Pausing, he took a breath and clearly made an effort to stifle another urge to smile. 'I'm fascinated, to be honest.'

'Most men find my work boring.' *Or threatening.*

'Perhaps you've been talking to the wrong men.'

Well, yes, Emily had discovered this the hard way, but she wasn't prepared to admit it now.

'I'd love to hear how you've done so well so quickly,' Jude prompted.

'By a rather roundabout route, to be honest.'

'The best stories are never straightforward.'

He managed to look genuinely interested, and Emily decided that Alex would be very pleased with his housemate's efforts to play the attentive host. At least talking about her job distracted her from other thoughts.

'The thing is, I never planned to work in a bank,' she said. 'I was always going to be a famous ballerina. After high school I went straight to Melbourne, to study ballet.'

'A dancer. That explains…' His voice tapered off.

'Explains what?'

'Why you're so graceful,' he said simply, but he looked unhappy, as if he wished he hadn't said that.

'I certainly loved everything about ballet. I loved the discipline, the music and the opportunities to perform. But—' she twisted the stem of her almost empty wine glass '—after a couple of years, I ran into problems with a choreographer.'

'A male choreographer?'

'Yes.' Looking up, her eyes met Jude's and she saw that he was watching her with another thoughtful frown.

'Let's just say I have bad luck with men.'

She let out a sigh. Just being here in Alex's kitchen reminded her of all the other times she'd been here, confiding in Alex. There was something about this setting, and the warm, exotic food and relaxing wine that seemed to encourage confidences.

And the man sitting opposite her might not be

Alex, but he had the loveliest smoky-grey eyes. Right now they looked soulful and understanding, almost as sympathetic as Alex's. Poor fellow. He felt obliged to fill Alex's shoes.

With a shrug, she found herself saying, 'When it comes to men, I make really bad choices. Or they make the bad choices. I don't know. I just know I always end up miserable and running away.'

'Is that what you're doing now?' Jude asked with surprising gentleness.

'Of course.' She lifted the glass and drained the last of her wine.

Then she jumped to her feet. 'Now, let me clean this up, seeing as you so kindly paid.'

'I won't argue with that.' He was on his feet, probably relieved to escape.

'And, Jude,' Emily said, as he turned to head out of the kitchen.

He turned back to her.

'I'll head off in the morning.'

His eyes grew cautious and he frowned again. 'Do you have somewhere to go?'

'I can easily find somewhere. I'll be fine. Coming here was a spur of the moment thing.

I had no idea Alex wasn't home. Tomorrow I'll leave you in peace.'

After a beat, he said, 'If you're sure.'

'I am, truly.'

It was totally silly of her to be disappointed when Jude nodded, then retreated, wishing her goodnight and muttering something about checking his emails.

Shortly afterwards, with the kitchen tidied, Emily went to Alex's room and, out of habit, she retrieved her phone from her bag. Almost immediately, she wished she hadn't bothered.

The first message was a text from a girlfriend in Wandabilla.

Is it really true about Michael? OMG. How awful.

Already, the gossip was spreading.

Emily's mind flashed to the photo she'd seen on Facebook just yesterday, a shot of Michael, her boyfriend of twelve months, with his pretty wife and two cute children, a little boy who looked just like him and a baby girl with golden curls.

Pain washed through her, an appalling tide of anguish and grief. How could he do that? She'd given him a whole year of her life, and she'd been ready to spend the rest of her life with him.

How could she have been such a fool?

CHAPTER TWO

NIGHTS were the worst for Jude. During the day, he could keep his thoughts under control and he wouldn't allow himself to worry. At night, however, the shadowy fears returned to haunt him, jumping out to snare him when he was almost asleep, or sneaking by the back door, sliding into his dreams.

Tonight, he came awake, shaking and drenched in a cold sweat, and he sat up quickly, hating the fact that waking brought very little comfort. His real life was almost as frightening as his dreams. His increasingly frequent headaches pointed to something serious, especially as lately his vision had begun to blur at the edges.

Alone at night, with no distractions, he found it so much harder to stop himself from worrying. This damn problem was dominating his life right now—even though he tried to hide it as best he could. All his life he'd viewed any ill-

ness as weakness—a bad habit he'd no doubt
learned from his father, who'd never had any
sympathy for their childhood illnesses. Measles,
flu, grazed knees…his dad had always made his
irritation very apparent.

Once, when Jude was about ten, he'd broken
his leg playing football.

'This will be a test of your manhood,' his father had said. 'Nobody likes a whinger.'

It was a message Jude had taken to heart.

Now, he noted the time—three-thirty a.m.—
which wasn't too bad. He'd already had several hours' sleep, and he only had to manage
for a few more hours before it would be day-
light again.

Rolling over, he closed his eyes and willed
himself to relax, but in the perfect stillness he
heard noises coming from down the hall.

Soft sounds of crying.

From Emily's room.

Any lingering thoughts about his own problems vanished. Jude sat up, listening intently
through the darkness. Emily's sobs were muffled, no doubt by her pillow, but, even so, the

crying went on and on in an uncontrollable out-
pouring of misery.

The sounds were like hammer blows to Jude's
conscience. He knew damn well that if Alex
were here Emily wouldn't be crying like this.
He'd promised Alex he'd keep an eye on her.

His feet hit the floor and he was halfway
across the room before his head caught up with
his chivalrous impulses.

OK. What, exactly, was he planning to do? Go
to Emily? Offer her a shoulder to cry on?

Brilliant. If she'd broken her heart over a good-
for-nothing boyfriend, she was hardly going to
welcome another lusty bloke offering to hold
her in his arms.

Sinking back onto the edge of his bed, Jude
remembered the way she'd looked at dinner as
she'd talked about her unhappy track record with
men. She'd seemed so fragile, with shadows beneath her eyes and a trembling droop to her soft
pink mouth. It was hard to believe she was the
same tough cookie who managed an entire district's bank accounts.

Obviously, the louse of a boyfriend had struck

a cruel blow, and she'd come here to recuperate. To be consoled by Alex.

Alex would have known how to help her. Alex would have listened and encouraged her to talk and he would have known, instinctively, what she needed. Whereas Jude felt utterly helpless and totally inadequate. To make matters worse, he'd more or less accepted her offer to leave, which was tantamount to booting her out of the door.

How lousy was that after he'd promised to look out for her?

At last the crying settled down, but Jude couldn't get back to sleep. He was in the kitchen quite early, brewing coffee, when Emily came into the room. In her nightgown.

Far out. He almost dropped the coffee pot. What was she thinking?

Her nightdress wasn't deliberately provocative or see-through, but the frothy concoction of cream and lace frills hinted at her nakedness underneath. And, with her red-gold hair tumbling about her pale shoulders, she looked like an old-fashioned princess, a young Elizabeth the First.

An appealing but tired princess who'd spent a troubled and anguished night.

Jude tried his best not to stare at the delightful hints of her breasts and bottom. He wondered if Emily assumed he was immune—gay, like Alex. He knew he should probably explain that this wasn't the case, but he wasn't sure how he could introduce the subject without tying himself in knots and embarrassing them both.

Instead, he tried to cover his reaction with an attempt at cheerfulness. 'Are you hungry?' he asked brightly. 'In the mood for pancakes? Or bacon and eggs?'

To his surprise, Emily made a shooing gesture. 'Don't worry about breakfast. I can look after it. You need to start your writing.'

'What are you? A slave-driver?' He smiled to indicate this was an attempt at humour.

Emily merely blinked. 'I thought you wrote madly all day and didn't bother about meals.'

Well, yes, he had given that impression last night, hadn't he? Truth was, he'd been writing since four a.m., and his hunger pangs had steadily mounted. For hours now he'd been fantasising about the breakfast ingredients they'd bought last night.

About to grab a frying pan, he saw, again, the red-rimmed despair in Emily's eyes, lingering traces of her midnight tears. She would probably find cheery chatter at breakfast painful. Perhaps the kindest thing he could offer was to stay clear and hide behind his work.

'I'll head off then,' he said quickly. 'But, before I go, I've been thinking about your plan to leave. You know there's no need.'

He couldn't quite believe he'd said that. The words had jumped out of nowhere.

Emily looked surprised, too. Her eyes widened and Jude almost back-pedalled. His life over the next week would be so much easier without her here.

'Are you sure, Jude?'

'Of course. You're Alex's cousin, and he wants to make his home welcome to you. You've more right to be here than I have.'

Her blue eyes sparkled with a suspicious sheen. 'That's very kind of you.'

Jude was quite sure he hadn't been half as kind

as Alex had hoped. He cleared his throat. 'And if you need to talk…'

To his dismay, Emily flushed brightly.

'I don't mean to pry,' he added awkwardly. 'I'm not Alex, but if there's any way I can help…'

'That's sweet of you, Jude, but I couldn't dump my problems onto you.'

He shrugged, unsure what to say. Counselling was so *not* his forte.

Then Emily gave a helpless flap of her hands. 'Oh, heck. Perhaps I should tell you what happened. Just to clear the air.'

He waited, leaning against the door jamb, trying to look as if he had all the time in the world.

'I've been seeing a geologist for over a year,' she said quietly but steadily. 'His name's Michael and he came to Wandabilla regularly as part of his work. Exploratory prospecting—that sort of thing. And—' she gave a hopeless little shrug '—he was charming and sexy and I fell in love…'

On the word *love* her voice cracked and she took another deep breath while her gaze was fixed on the jug of yellow daffodils on the kitchen counter.

'This week, Michael and I were supposed to go away on holiday together. I'd taken my annual leave. Everything was planned.'

Again Emily paused, paying serious attention to the daffodils. 'We were due to fly to Fiji, but on the night before our flight, a friend sent me a link to a Facebook page. Actually, it was a link to Michael's *wife's* Facebook page.'

Suddenly, her mouth twisted out of shape.

Jude's throat tightened. 'You're absolutely sure it was him?' he asked, keeping any hint of reproach from his voice.

Emily nodded. 'Michael admitted it. He could hardly deny it when the photo was there on the screen. There he was with his lovely wife and two beautiful children. They live in South Australia and his name's not even Michael. It's Mark.'

Jude's hands fisted, itching to land a punch on the rat's nose.

'So that's my sad little story.' Emily's lips tilted in a travesty of a smile. 'But please don't worry. I'm OK. Heartbreak's not fatal. I'll get over it.'

'But you must stay here as long as you need

to,' Jude said. 'Try not to take any notice of me. Just treat this place as your own.'

'Well, if you're sure…thanks.'

He raised his coffee mug in a salute, and managed to smile. 'I'll be off to the salt mines, but I might sneak back later to make some toast.'

'Oh, I can make toast for you.' Suddenly she was eager, as if to make amends. 'What would you like on it? Marmalade? A slice of bacon?'

'Ah—bacon would be great. Thank you.'

'Actually,' she said with a hopeful look, 'I make a great bacon sandwich.'

'Sounds terrific.'

As Jude retreated to his room, he told himself that keeping his distance from Emily was, truly, his wisest option. She needed privacy to get over her heartache, and he had plenty of reasons to keep to himself.

Reasons he preferred not to think about now. But the appointment at the hospital was looming towards him like headlights on a speeding freight train. Every time he thought about the tests and the possible outcome, he was flooded by a rush of anxiety.

Shaking those thoughts aside, he opened his

work in progress, and he prayed that his muse would be friendly, letting him escape into a world of fantasy.

The words did not flow.

Not the right words, at any rate. Jude's morning commenced poorly and came to a grinding halt when Emily, still in her nightdress, appeared at his door with a tray.

'Breakfast,' she said softly, as if she were afraid to interrupt a genius at work.

The tray held the promised bacon sandwich, which smelled amazing, as well as a glass of freshly squeezed orange juice and another pot of coffee.

'My ministering angel,' he told her and she gave a self-conscious laugh.

'Hardly.'

'Well, in that get-up, you look like some kind of angel.'

She blushed and looked upset and Jude immediately wished he could take the words back. Too late, she was already whirling away and he found himself watching her retreating heels, flashing pink beneath the frilled hem of her nightdress.

He didn't see her again for the rest of the day. Which was, he decided, a very good thing.

Naturally he was grateful that he'd been left in peace. Except…the afternoon's writing fared as badly as the morning's. Ideas wouldn't come. Words evaded Jude and when he emerged from his room at the end of the day, he felt particularly irritable and sluggish. And mad with himself for wasting precious hours.

Usually, when he felt like this, he went for a long, brisk walk to shake out the cobwebs. This evening, however, he was distracted by enticing aromas wafting from the kitchen.

Following his nose, he discovered Emily wrapped in one of Alex's gaudy aprons, and looking especially fetching with her bright hair pinned up in a loose knot from which fiery tendrils escaped.

'That smells amazing.'

She turned to him and she was a bit pink and flushed, but much happier than she'd been when she'd left his office this morning. In fact, she sent him a bright-eyed smile. 'It's coq au vin. I hope you like it.'

'I'm sure I'll love it, but I don't expect you to cook for me, Emily.'

'I don't mind. I like cooking, and it's my way of repaying you for last night's dinner.' She shot him a quick enquiring glance. 'Or were you planning to go out?'

It occurred to Jude that he should have called one of his mates and planned an evening out. Surely that was a wiser plan than spending another night at home with this far too attractive girl.

However, he found himself saying, 'I don't have any plans.' And he helped himself to a glass of iced water from the fridge. 'That dinner smells sensational.'

'So speaks a self-confessed pushover when it comes to food.'

'Sprung,' he admitted with a rueful smile.

Emily smiled, too, and he thought he could stare at her smile for ever…

'I've tried to keep quiet,' she said. 'Have you had a productive day?'

'Not very.'

For a moment she looked worried, but then her eyes widened with unmistakable excitement. 'I bought one of your novels this afternoon. It's called *Thorn in the Flesh* and I've started reading it. It's fabulous, Jude. Totally gripping. I'm hooked, and it's exactly what I needed to stop me from dwelling…on…everything.'

'I'm glad it hit the spot.'

To his surprise, she folded her arms and leant a shapely hip against a kitchen cupboard with the air of someone settling in for a discussion. 'Morgan, the heroine, is really tough,' she said. 'Mentally tough. And I like the way she guards her heart.' Emily rolled her eyes. 'I should be more like her.'

Jude shrugged. 'Perhaps you're too hard on yourself. Fictional characters are always larger than life.'

'That's true, I guess.'

'I could never live up to my hero's standards.'

She nodded. 'Raff's a very cool customer, isn't he?'

'Of course.'

Of course… Jude thought. His heroes had always been very cool and very tough, ever since he'd first created them for the stories he told to his little sister, Charlotte. At the age of eight he'd been trying to drown out the nightly ordeal of their parents' rowdy arguments.

These days, with new enemies, Jude wished it was as easy to escape from reality.

Emily had turned to the stove and was adjusting the flame beneath the fragrantly simmering pot. 'Have you heard from Alex?' she asked casually.

'Not today.'

'Do you miss him?' She gave the pot a stir.

Finishing his iced water, Jude shrugged. 'Not especially. He'll only be away for three weeks or so.'

Then he saw the way Emily was watching him, her blue eyes soft and round with obvious sympathy, and he realised with a slam of dismay that she'd decided he was Alex's lover.

He should deny it now. Tell her the truth. Hell, just looking at her in her simple jeans and Alex's striped apron, Jude was fighting off desire so strong that it startled him. He was surprised that Emily could stand there in the same room and not be aware of his screaming lust.

Thing was, it should have been dead easy to

set her straight. How hard was it to make a simple statement? *By the way, Emily, I'm not gay.*

All things being equal, he would have told her. Immediately. No problem.

Except…there were other factors at play here. Emily was enjoying a kind of immunity in this apartment, but if she knew the truth about him, she was likely to pick up on the attraction he felt. For all kinds of reasons, that was a bad idea.

Her trust in men had taken a severe hammering and she'd come here seeking sanctuary. Feeling safe was very important to her right now, and Jude didn't want to upset that. This apartment offered her time-out. From men. Time to pick up the pieces after her recent relationship disaster. The last thing she needed was an awareness of a new guy with the hots for her.

Just as importantly, Jude knew he was totally crazy to entertain randy thoughts when he'd come to the city to find out what the hell was wrong with him. He needed a medical diagnosis, not a romantic entanglement with the first gorgeous girl who walked through the door.

All things considered, it was much easier and

safer to simply let Emily assume that he was gay. After all, she wouldn't be here for long, and he—

Hell. He had his life on hold until he knew what the future had in store for him.

When Emily woke the next morning she felt marginally happier. She'd slept quite well during the night, no doubt because she'd gone to bed feeling thoroughly relaxed after a pleasant evening at home with Jude.

They'd enjoyed a leisurely meal, which Jude had complimented lavishly, and then they'd sunk into comfy armchairs and read novels in the pleasantly heated lounge room while CDs played softly in the background. It had been rather cosy and undemanding, the kind of evening she'd often spent with Alex.

Now, having dressed in jeans and a sweater because she didn't want another comment about angels and nightgowns, she wandered into the kitchen at almost nine o'clock. It was the longest sleep she'd had in ages. No wonder she felt better.

To her surprise, there were no signs that Jude was up. The kettle was cold, which meant he'd either made his cuppa long ago, or he hadn't bothered.

She made coffee and blueberry pancakes and assembled a breakfast tray, as she had on the previous day, then knocked softly on Jude's door. After all, bringing him breakfast was the least she could do when he was hard at work and generously sharing his living space with her.

He didn't answer to her knock, which was another surprise. She wondered if he was in some kind of artistic frenzy, typing madly as the clever words flowed straight from his imagination through his fingertips and onto the keyboard. He might be very angry if she interrupted.

Then again…he'd welcomed the breakfast she'd prepared yesterday. She knocked again, less cautiously this time.

There was a muffled growl from inside.

'Jude, would you like coffee and pancakes?'

At first he didn't answer, but then the door opened slowly and Jude leant a bulky shoulder against the door frame. He was wearing black boxer shorts and a holey grey T-shirt that hugged his muscly arms and chest. His eyes

were squinted as if the muted light in the hallway was too bright.

His dark hair was tousled into rough spikes,
his jaw covered in a thin layer of dark stubble,
but it was the glassy strain in his eyes that told
Emily he was in pain.

'I won't bother with breakfast this morning,'
he said dully. Then, added as an afterthought,
'Thanks, those pancakes look great, but I'm not
hungry.'

'Are you unwell?'

'Headache.'

'Oh, gosh, I'm sorry. Is there anything I can
get you? Do you need aspirin? Camomile tea?'

A ghost of a smile flitted over his face and he
started to shake his head, then grimaced, as if
the movement was too painful. 'I have medica-
tion. Don't worry, I'm used to this. I'll hit the
sack for an hour or so and then I should be fine.'

Clearly, Jude didn't want to be bothered by any
more questions, so Emily tiptoed away, leaving
him to rest, but she felt disturbed and worried.
She'd experienced guys with hangovers, but Jude
hadn't been drinking, and he'd said he was used
to these headaches. How awful for him.

A pool of morning sunlight on the balcony beckoned, so, feeling unaccountably subdued, she ate her breakfast at a little wrought-iron-and-glass table, with *Thorn in the Flesh* propped against a pot plant. She finished the last two chapters while she ate.

Jude's story was wonderful. Not only was there a fabulously thrilling chase at the end to catch the bad guys, but there was also a lovely and poignant romantic finale for the deserving hero and heroine. She marvelled that a gay man could portray the male-female emotions so perfectly.

There was only one problem. When Emily put the book down, she came back to earth with an abrupt and unhappy thud. Her own romances had never finished happily. Every one of them had ended suddenly and miserably, leaving her to feel like The World's Greatest Romantic Loser.

She couldn't help wondering if there was something crucially wrong with her personality. Some genetic defect that caused her to always fall for the wrong man.

All she wanted, really, was to be like her parents, to find one person to love, one relationship to feel safe inside. She'd grown up watching their warmth and affection and she'd listened many times to their story of how they'd met at a country dance and married young, never regretting their decision.

Even her brother Jack had been lucky in love. He'd married his high school sweetheart, Kelly, a girl from a nearby farm. There'd only ever been one girl for Jack, and now he and Kelly were ridiculously happy.

Emily's family made finding love look easy, and yet she'd tried so many times and failed. Now, she punished herself with memories, starting with Dimitri, the dark and ruggedly handsome Russian choreographer at the ballet school in Melbourne.

Having taken advantage of her youth and naivety, Dimitri had promptly dropped her overnight when he took up with one of the stars of the Australian Ballet. Emily had taken almost a year to recover from that heartbreak.

Back home in the Wandabilla district, she'd met Dave, a nice, safe farmer, and this time she was sure she'd struck gold. She would marry and live on a farm near her family, and she could envision her happy future so easily.

Dave had been as different from Dimitri as possible—practical and rough around the edges, and not the slightest bit interested in 'culture'. She'd been happy to swap satin pointe shoes and the barre for tractors and cow manure.

But Dave's first love was rodeos and, eventually, he'd taken off on the competition circuit, travelling to all the outback events. He'd expected Emily to throw up her job and follow him, but she wasn't prepared to do that, she'd realised, much to her own surprise.

In western New South Wales, Dave had discovered Annie, a camp-drafting champion who shared his passion, and his phone calls to Emily had stopped.

After that, Emily had thrown herself into her work. She'd attended workshops on customer relations and marketing, and any other professional development programmes that could boost her up the corporate ladder.

When she'd dived into the dating pool—unsurprisingly, it was rather shallow in Wandabilla— she'd set herself strict rules. No longer would she be so trusting and open, and she wouldn't allow herself to fall in love again until she met a man who ticked all the right boxes. Following her new plan, she'd never gone out with any one fellow more than a few times, and she was determined from then on that *she* would be the one who ended her relationships.

She had been feeling quite confident again. Before Michael had arrived in town.

Conservatively good-looking, intelligent and charming, Michael had been perfect. Emily had learned from her mistakes, however, and she'd resisted his attention at first. Michael had chased her with flattering persistence and, in the end, she'd decided he was genuine in his admiration.

And surely he was safe? He wasn't a foreign artist or an outback drifter. He wasn't even a local. He was a geologist from South Australia, prospecting in the Wandabilla district for a mining company.

Admittedly, Michael was only in her district for six weeks at a time, but he flew back regularly, and he always wrote to her or phoned her while he was away.

In time she was confident that he was *The One*.

After all, weren't geologists clever and educated, and as solid and dependable as the rocks they studied?

What a joke.

Emily let out a long groan of frustration. And pain.

Losing Michael hurt. So much. Her pain went way beyond disappointment. She felt betrayed, used and foolish, as if she hadn't gained one single jot of wisdom since Dimitri. And, even though she was the innocent party, she felt guilty that she'd slept with someone else's husband and father.

She could too easily imagine how deeply Michael—no, *Mark's*—wife loved him, could imagine how hurt the other woman would be if she ever found out.

Emily's sense of gloom dived even deeper when she returned to the kitchen and saw the blinking light on her mobile phone.

Wincing at the possibilities, she clicked on her message bank and discovered five—count them, *five*—new text messages from people in Wandabilla.

Normally, she would try to reply, to at least thank these people for their concern, even though they weren't genuinely close friends but mainly curious gossipers.

Today, however, there were also three voice messages from Michael-slash-Mark, and his first message was full of apologies and entreaties, begging her to ring him back.

Hearing his voice brought a fresh slug of misery and anger, and Emily almost hurled the phone across the room.

She might have done that, actually, if she wasn't worried that the crash would wake Jude. Her gaze flashed to his novel, *Thorn in the Flesh*, sitting on the breakfast tray, and she remembered Morgan, Jude's tough heroine.

Emily needed to be like her. From now on.

Smiling, she picked up the phone and deleted every single message without responding.

It felt good.

Very good, actually.

CHAPTER THREE

Mid-afternoon...

EMILY had been out to a bookshop, where she'd bought two more of Jude's books, and she was stretched out on the sofa, deeply absorbed in a thrilling mystery set in the wilds of The Kimberley Coast when she heard Jude's door open. Shortly after, she heard the sound of the shower in the bathroom.

Good. He must be feeling better. She was surprised by how pleased she felt about this. She even found her attention wandering from the book as she waited for Jude to emerge from the bathroom. It was suddenly important to make sure that he really was OK.

When he finally came into the living room, freshly shaved, hair damp from the shower and smelling pleasantly of lemon-scented soap, he was no longer frowning or squinting with pain, and it was almost impossible to tell that he'd been unwell.

'Feeling better?' Emily asked with a jolly-nurse smile.

'Much better, thanks.' He seemed keen to shrug her concern aside. 'Actually, I'm heading out now.'

It was crazy to be instantly disappointed. Why should she miss Jude? She'd never been a person who was needy for company.

Annoyed with herself, she held up the book she was reading. 'I'm really enjoying this, by the way.'

Jude saw the cover and his eyes glinted with amusement. 'Don't tell me I've acquired a fan?'

'Perhaps,' she said airily. 'You've done a good job with Ellie. She has hang-ups like the rest of us, but she wouldn't dare let them show. I like that about her. She's classy. And I love that she's blonde and leggy and carries a pistol in her handbag.'

'Glad you approve.' Hands sunk deep in the pockets of his jeans, Jude bowed with mock so-lemnity, then turned and headed for the door.

'Don't worry about dinner,' he called over his shoulder. 'It's my turn to cook tonight.'

Emily was about to remind him that he didn't like to cook when he looked back and she caught the ghost of a twinkle in his eye.

'How about I bring home Thai?' he said, then quickly disappeared before she could answer.

The front door closed behind him, and the apartment felt weirdly empty.

It was quite late, almost dark, when Jude arrived back bearing the promised tubs of take-away Thai. They ate on the balcony, watching the last of the sunset over distant Mount Coot-tha.

'I was wondering if you'd like to see a movie tonight,' he asked as they ate. 'It'll cheer us both up.'

'Do we need cheering up?'

He sent her a measuring glance. 'Isn't that why you're here?'

'Well, yes,' she admitted. 'But I'm not your responsibility, Jude. Don't feel obliged to entertain me.'

'I could do with cheering, too. That blasted headache left me feeling a bit out of sorts.'

'That's not surprising.' Emily couldn't shake off the lingering suspicion that there was something else, something more deeply serious that was troubling him. She didn't know him well enough to ask, so she said instead, 'I suppose you'd prefer to see a thriller?'

'Would you mind?' He offered her an apologetic shrug. 'I've never been much good with chick flicks.'

'That surprises me, actually. I thought you must watch them and study them. You write such lovely romantic scenes in your books.'

'Do I?' He looked suddenly caught out, almost guilty.

'But don't worry,' Emily assured him. 'I'm happy to watch a thriller. I'm certainly not in the mood for romance.'

This time when their gazes met, she thought she caught a different expression—a momentary flash in Jude's handsome grey eyes that caught her completely on the back foot. Not at all what she'd expected from a gay man. For a moment, she'd gained the unlikely impression that he was very much aware of her—as a woman.

Heaven knew she'd read that message in men's eyes often enough in the past. But surely she was being fanciful now? Of all the guys she'd spent time with, Jude was safe.

To her relief, he said simply, 'A thriller it is then. There's a really good one that just came out last week. And it will be my shout. After all, I get to count it as research.'

It was certainly pleasant to get out of the house, to wrap up and walk the frosty streets, and it was nice to know she could enjoy a man's company without any danger of breaking her heart.

The movie, as Jude had predicted, was an exciting, edge-of-the-seat thriller, and it soon worked its magic. For close to two hours Emily almost stopped thinking about Michael.

Joy.

'I definitely feel better for having seen that,' she said as they left the cinema.

Jude raised a questioning eyebrow. 'Do you want to prolong the fun? Are you in a rush to get home, or would you like to find somewhere for coffee?'

Going back to the apartment would mean returning to her solitary bedroom and her solitary one-track thoughts.

'I'd love to stay out for a bit longer,' she admitted. 'I'm glad you seem to have completely recovered.'

'So am I.' He smiled, but the effect was spoiled by the flicker of a shadow in his eyes. 'I'm fine now.'

Emily wished she hadn't seen that flicker. For a fanciful second it had looked like the shadow of a falling axe. She wished she could shake off the sense that something was really troubling Jude, and she wondered if he was trying to distract himself, just as she was. It was probably a good thing she'd agreed to stay out.

They found a snug table in the back corner of a crowded coffee shop. Emily ordered hot chocolate, which came with tiny pink and white marshmallows for melting, and Jude ordered tea—Lapsang Souchong, which arrived in a ruby-glass pot, smelling smoky and inexplicably masculine.

'You drink the same tea as your hero, Raff,' she teased as she scooped a sticky blob of marshmallow from her mug.

Jude smiled. 'Strange coincidence, isn't it?'

As they sipped their warm drinks, they talked about the movie, debating the significance of some of the plot twists.

'The scriptwriters certainly knew all about crime and the underbelly of society,' Emily suggested. Across the lamplit table, she narrowed her eyes at Jude. 'So do you, actually. It shows in your books. How do you do it? How do you get inside the mind of a hardened criminal?'

'I research,' he answered simply.

'Yes, I guessed that, but *how*? Who do you talk to?'

'Hardened criminals.'

He said this so dryly and with such a poker face that, momentarily, she almost fell for it.

Then, matching his dry tone, she replied. 'So you're telling me it's not safe to associate with you.'

This time his eyes twinkled. 'Touché. Of course, you're safe.'

There was a moment, as their gazes met across

the table, when Emily felt a kind of woozy warmth that was totally unfitting.

'Seriously,' she said abruptly, shaking off the feeling. 'I'm interested in how you make your stories so real.'

'Seriously,' Jude said, 'I have contacts with the police and in the military. I've grilled them mercilessly about their work. I've spent full days with a firearms instructor, and another day observing Army commando training. I've even taken part, so I know what it feels like to be cuffed, down on the ground and immobile while a tactical unit performs a mock hostage rescue.'

With a smile, he said, 'And now I've met a bank manager, and that could be very handy, too. I can imagine all sorts of scenarios involving a heist and a beautiful banking boss.'

Heat flamed in Emily's cheeks, and she pressed her hands against the patches of warmth, hoping to hide them. She couldn't believe she was blushing simply because Jude had implied she was beautiful. Of all the ridiculous reactions.

Why should she blush over this man's completely non-sexual assessment of her looks?

To cover her silly reaction, she made a joke

against herself. 'Just my luck, one of the robbers will turn out to be a former boyfriend.' Then, quickly, she steered the subject safely away from herself. 'What about your current book? Where's it set?'

'The Gold Coast. But I'm beginning to think it's a bit too close to home. I prefer more distant settings.'

'Why? Does your imagination work better at a distance?'

He looked at her with surprise. 'Yes, I think it does.' Then he frowned. 'Are you pretending to be interested, or are you genuinely curious?'

'I'm genuine. Honestly. Why do you ask?'

Jude shook his head. 'I was just wondering… I wouldn't have expected a bank manager to be interested in fiction.'

'You're stereotyping,' she accused with rather more iciness than she actually felt.

'Yeah. It's a failing.' Jude's unrepentant gaze flickered over her and then swept around the crowded café and the chattering customers gathered in the booths. 'I know it's not polite to mention this, but your clothes seem very—or should

I say—*extremely* fashionable. Not quite what I'd expected from a little place like Wandabilla.'

'Is this another example of your narrow views?'

'I'm afraid it is.' He confessed this without a hint of remorse. 'But I'm genuinely curious. Is it a status thing?'

'I...I suppose it might be.' Emily hadn't been asked this question before, but there were a lot of wealthy farmers who conducted their business at her bank and classy clothes had become her armour. For a young woman to hang on to a position of power, she had to win respect any way she could.

At least, this was what she'd told herself, but she sometimes wondered if her efforts to acquire a perfect career and a perfect wardrobe were compensation for her lack of a perfect relationship.

'So where do you shop?' Jude asked. 'Do you travel to the city?'

'Not often. I do almost all my shopping online.' She gave a little laugh. 'I love the Internet. If I ever give up my current job, I think I'll develop some kind of business I can run online.'

Thinking about the Internet, however, brought back sickening memories of Michael-slash-Mark.

Emily wasn't sure how long she sat there, sunk in miserable memories.

Eventually, she heard Jude's voice.

'Are you OK?'

He asked this solicitously, just as Alex might have, and she couldn't help answering honestly. 'I'm very mad with myself for wasting a whole year on a relationship that was never going anywhere.'

'It's not easy to see through a practised conman. They're usually consummate charmers.' Jude's face was surprisingly fierce. 'My father was like that—having affairs all over the place.'

His hands were clenched into fists on the tabletop. 'And then my mother punished him by having revenge affairs.'

He looked so upset, Emily stopped thinking about her own worries. She was imagining Jude growing up with unhappy parents. At least her problems hadn't started until she'd left home.

Their conversation, she realised, had suddenly gone deeper. Jude's grey eyes were as hard as granite, as if just thinking about his parents changed him completely.

'Have you ever talked to Alex about this?' she asked.

Jude looked startled. 'No.'

'It's just that he's very good at laying ghosts to rest.'

'Yes, I can imagine he would be.' Then Jude gave a shake, as if ridding himself of unwanted memories.

They lapsed into silence and Emily finished off her chocolate. 'I'm sure I have a moustache.' With an embarrassed smile, she reached for a paper napkin.

'Here, let me.'

To her surprise, Jude took the napkin from her and dabbed at her upper lip. The pressure of his fingers so close to her mouth felt strangely intimate and he was looking at her with an intensity that stole her breath.

After what felt like an age, he blinked like someone coming out of a trance, then dropped the napkin onto his saucer. 'What were we talking about?'

Emily's mind had gone blank. To her dismay,

she found herself thinking how attractive he was, and how the message in his grey eyes had made her feel strangely knife-edgy and weight-less. And there was a vibe between them, an impossible awareness that was very confusing.

Surely her imagination was playing tricks on her? There must be something wrong with her. After her debacle with Michael, she couldn't possibly be interested in *any* man for ages. Right now, a life of celibacy had huge appeal and, any-way, Jude wasn't even available.

She made a flustered, helpless gesture, hoping to break the strange spell that seemed to have fallen over her, and promptly knocked the pep-per pot. Next moment she was sneezing, then floundering in her bag for tissues.

Fortunately, after she'd finished blowing her nose, Jude suggested it was time to leave. Emily gratefully agreed.

Outside, it was chillier than ever. She turned up her collar and sunk her hands deep into her warm coat pockets, and hoped that the cold night air would clear her head of nonsense. She walked beside Jude in sober silence, wondering what on earth he was thinking. Had he noticed her silly reaction?

They didn't talk on the way back, for which she was grateful, and when she stole glimpses in Jude's direction, he seemed to be frowning and thoughtful. So it was a surprise when they reached the apartment that he turned to her with a warm smile.

'Thanks for a great night.'

'Thank *you*,' she said politely. 'It was a good idea to go out tonight. Just what I needed.'

'Same here.'

Despite the formality of their exchange, they stood in the hallway, neither one moving, as if they were trapped again by a mysterious spell. But the last thing—the *very last thing*—Emily expected was that Jude would lean in and kiss her.

On the lips.

And yet he did just that.

Before she had time to think, he was holding her by the shoulders and he was kissing her effortlessly and expertly. So expertly that she forgot to be shocked at first. She was seduced by the enticing smell of him and the warm, blissful pressure of his lips. Instinctively, she closed her eyes and gave in to the deliciousness of the moment.

An inappropriate stretch of time elapsed before she remembered that this kiss was wrong.

Wrong, wrong, wrong, wrong, wrong!

For heaven's sake.

She sprang back in shocked horror.

How had this happened? Had her brain short-circuited? Stunned, she pressed her fingers to her tingling lips. 'That was…unexpected.'

Understatement of the year.

'I'm sorry,' Jude said. 'I couldn't help it. You're so lovely.'

'And…' She gasped as the bald truth became obvious. 'And you're not gay.'

'No,' he said softly. 'I'm not.'

Gathering her dignity and her anger about her like a protective cape, she glared at him. 'You conned me, Jude. You pretended to be safe and uninterested in women. You let me assume you were like Alex, so I was lulled into a false sense of security.'

'I'm sorry, Emily. I—'

She cut him off with an angry cry, then

stamped her foot. 'I should have known that every male on this planet is a scheming, cheating rat.'

Anger and despair swept through her. She was reliving Michael's deception. She'd trusted Michael utterly.

Now, she'd trusted Jude to be a safe, uncomplicated friend, but he was as bad as every other man.

Beyond furious, she raised her hand and slapped him hard.

Whirling around, she marched down the hallway to her room, kicking the door savagely behind her. *Bang! Slam!*

Jude winced as Emily's door crashed shut.

Good one, Marlowe.

What on earth had possessed him to kiss Emily? Had a kind of madness overcome him?

It was his only explanation.

He'd spent an entire evening in her company and she'd been lovely and amusing and interesting—in other words, utterly enchanting. On the walk home, the crisp night air had heightened her loveliness even further, adding stars to her eyes and colour to her cheeks and lips, and he'd been spellbound. Totally. He hadn't been able to resist stealing one little kiss.

He hadn't meant to shock her. He'd imagined that at some stage during this evening she'd guessed that he found her impossibly attractive.

That wasn't a good enough excuse, was it?

Damn.

Emily had come here for security and, while he hadn't actually lied to her, he'd held back the truth that he and Alex were nothing more than friends and business associates. And *of course* he should have shown more restraint just now. He should have known that Emily's sense of trust was too fragile to mess with. For goodness' sake, she was only a few days out of another relationship!

Problem was—he'd been looking for a distraction tonight, looking for anything to help him forget the barrage of tests he'd undergone at the hospital this afternoon. Tomorrow morning he would find out the results of these procedures and he would no doubt learn the cause of the headaches and vision problems that had plagued him over the past few months.

Truth be told, he was horrified. His career and, possibly, his life hung on the edge of a precipice.

Tonight had been all about forgetting—warding off fear, holding back the future.

But he'd been selfish. Of course he had.

He knew what Emily had been through. He knew she had trust issues—and, in all honesty, he'd known she'd thought he was gay. His health issues weren't a good enough excuse for helping himself to a kiss that hadn't been on offer.

Nor was the fact that he found her loveliness irresistible. He wasn't the first guy who'd had that problem.

Emily lay awake for ages, stewing over men's dishonesty.

The knowledge that she'd once again been hoodwinked was almost more than she could bear.

But, despite her anger, she was beginning to suspect that perhaps she shouldn't have hit Jude. She felt rather guilty remembering the way her hand had stung, which meant his face must have stung even more.

He'd been rather manly about it, not even

flinching, even though he must have seen the slap coming.

He'd taken it on the cheek and, at the time, she'd thought, *Good. Serve him right.*

Now she was beginning to suspect that she'd hadn't really been hitting out at Jude, but at Michael. Michael-slash-Mark. So, along with her anger, she now had to deal with guilt, too. Heavens, she was Jude's guest, and she couldn't start a habit of slapping every guy who tried to kiss her.

It was ages before she drifted off to sleep, but in the end she slept deeply and woke quite late.

She took her time getting up, thinking at first that Jude could get his own breakfast this morning. But when she tried to resurrect the previous night's anger, she found that it had weakened. Granny Silver had always told her that things looked different after a good night's sleep and, more than once, her grandmother had been right.

Now, Emily felt guiltier than ever about her over-the-top reaction to Jude's kiss. It hadn't been a demanding kiss, after all, even though it had felt surprisingly intimate. Surely, she could have handled it more wisely and coolly?

She knew very well that a girl who didn't want to be kissed shouldn't stand in a hallway, smiling dreamily into smouldering grey eyes.

In the clear light of morning, she decided that there was no point in sulking. Jude had been very good about sharing this apartment with her and she just had to remember to be ultra-cautious in future. More head than heart—like Jude's heroines.

At least, after last night's carry-on, Jude wouldn't want to repeat the kiss, so hopefully they could resume their friendship without any drama. She would suggest something to that effect at breakfast.

By the time Emily had showered and dressed, however, she discovered that Jude had long gone. The door to his room was wide open and she could see that his bed was made, his laptop closed and his desk was uncharacteristically tidy.

In the kitchen the kettle was lukewarm, as if it had been boiled some time ago, and there was a mug with a coffee ring and a plate with a smattering of toast crumbs in the sink.

It was rather frustrating. Emily had been ready to talk to Jude, to clear the air. Disappointed, she went back to her room to switch on her phone and check for messages. Even a nosy text from Wandabilla would be welcome right now, but there was something better—a voice message from her grandmother.

It was wonderful to hear her granny's familiar musical voice and Emily rang straight back. 'Granny, I'm sorry I missed your call.'

'That's all right, dear. I was just ringing to let you know that I'm coming down to Brisbane today. I have an appointment at the hospital.'

'Not for anything serious, I hope.'

'No, thank goodness. It's my six-month check-up after my cataract operation.'

'Oh, that's all right then. What time's your appointment? I can meet you at the hospital, then take you to lunch.'

'Oh, Emily, I'd love that. Thank you.'

'Me, too. I'm looking forward to it already.'

Emily didn't like hospitals—they were so huge and clinical and grim. When she arrived at the ophthalmology department, she was told that her grandmother was still being attended to, so she sat in the waiting area thumbing through a very

out-of-date magazine. She wished she'd remembered to bring Jude's book to read.

There was plenty of action about the place, of
course, plenty of people in white coats and always someone coming or going. Emily passed
the time by people-watching, which she'd always
found fascinating, although she'd learned not to
trust first impressions.

In her job, many, many people walked into her
office, and she knew very well that their exte-
rior appearance was not always a true indica-
tor of the health of their bank accounts, or the
strength of their character.

Pity she never remembered this when it came
to her love life.

She was mulling this over and flipping idly
through the magazine when firm footsteps on
the polished linoleum caught her attention. She
looked up to see, of all people, Jude.

He was striding down the corridor, looking pale and worried. When he saw Emily, he
stopped abruptly, and looked as shocked to see
her as she was to see him.

'What are you doing here?' His expression was
one of worry, mingled with something close to

horror. 'Are you following me? This is none of your business, Emily.'

'I've come to collect my grandmother. She's having her eyes checked.'

'Oh, right.' The furrows in Jude's brow lessened marginally, as did the anguish in his eyes.

'But what about you, Jude? You seem upset.'

His throat rippled as he swallowed, and for a moment he looked as if he didn't want to answer her. He looked away, and his jaw squared and tightened as he stared hard at something down the corridor.

Remembering his awful headache yesterday, Emily was pierced by a nasty suspicion, but then his expression eased back into his usual good humour.

'I'm fine.' He gave her a disarming smile. 'I've been having my eyes tested, too. I need a new prescription for my reading glasses, for working at the computer.'

'Oh, is that all?' She found herself releasing a huff of relief. 'For a minute there you had me worried that it was something serious. That headache yesterday really knocked you out.'

'No doubt because I need the new glasses,' he

said with a casual shrug. 'But thanks for your concern.' With a cautious smile, he added, 'Does this mean you're no longer mad at me?'

At the memory of last night's kiss and its aftermath, Emily blushed, much to her consternation.

'I guess not.' She spoke frostily to counteract the blush but, in truth, she *was* more than a little ashamed of last night's overreaction. 'I'm prepared to call a truce.'

'A truce?' Jude's right eyebrow hiked high. 'Does that involve terms and conditions?'

'Most definitely.' Emily shot a quick glance about her and was dismayed to discover that several people in the waiting area were watching them with acute interest. 'We can sort out the details later,' she said, lowering her voice.

'I'll look forward to it,' Jude replied in a low rumbling tone that set unacceptable vibrations thrumming inside her.

Perhaps it was just as well that her grandmother appeared then, full of smiles.

'Granny, how'd you go?'

'Wonderfully.' Granny Silver beamed at them. 'My eyes are better than they've been in a decade.'

'How fabulous.' Emily gave her a hug, but

as soon as she released her grandmother, the elderly woman turned her attention to Jude. Introductions were necessary, and then explanations. 'Jude is a writer, Granny. He writes under his own name—Jude Marlowe—and Alex is his agent.'

'And I'm very pleased to meet you, Mrs Silver. Both Emily and Alex have spoken so highly of you.'

'Have they really?' Granny laughed and sent Jude a flirtatious sideways smile. 'Now, I do hope you're going to join us for lunch, Jude.'

'Sorry. I'd love to, but not today.'

'What a pity. I assumed you came here to meet up with Emily. Are you terribly busy?'

Emily had been watching Jude during this exchange and she thought she'd caught an underlying tension beneath the surface warmth and politeness. She was sure he was still worried about something, but trying to hide it.

'Why don't you join us?' she asked him on an impulse she didn't quite understand. No doubt it was her conscience urging her to make up for slapping him last night. 'Lunch won't take up too much of your time, and you'll still have all the afternoon for your writing.'

Jude's eyes shimmered with an unreadable emotion. 'Is this part of your truce deal?'

'It might as well be.'

'It's very kind, Emily, but I—'

'Oh, come on,' urged Granny as she sensed Jude's hesitation. 'It's not often that I have the chance to enjoy lunch in the company of a handsome young man.'

'How could I refuse such a flattering invitation?' he replied gallantly. 'In any case, I have my car here, so I can offer you a lift.'

'Wonderful,' said Granny.

They dined at Granny's favourite Italian restaurant overlooking the Brisbane River. There was no problem arranging for an extra place to be set at their table in a sunny corner with a view. Granny was charming company, as always, and Jude seemed to relax as he basked in the warmth of her smile.

He even turned on the charm as they ate their delicious meals—veal Marsala for Granny, mushroom risotto for Emily and gnocchi Gorgonzola for Jude. As soon as he discovered that Granny

Silver was a great bird-lover, he chatted animatedly about sightings of terns and honeyeaters, parrots and bowerbirds. The old lady was delighted.

For Emily, it was all very pleasant, sitting in a stream of gentle winter sunshine, joining in the agreeable conversation while looking out at the boats on the river and the elegant houses lining the far bank. She was reminded of the many happy times she and Alex had dined with their granny. Pleasant memories were important—they helped counteract all the bad ones.

As they were finishing their coffee, Jude rose and excused himself. Moments later, Emily saw him talking to the cashier and realised that he was already paying the bill.

'This was supposed to be my shout,' she protested, rising from her seat.

She was stopped by a bony hand on her arm. 'Don't fret, Emily. If it bothers you, you can always talk to Jude about it later.'

'I guess…'

'Why not let your grandmother enjoy a little old-fashioned largesse from a nice-looking man?'

As Emily sat down again, both women watched

the tall, dark figure on the far side of the room while he shared a smiling exchange with the girl at the till.

'He's just the kind of man you need,' Granny Silver said in a confiding tone.

'No. Don't start that, Granny.'

For long seconds her grandmother studied her, a shrewdly measuring light gleaming in her lively blue eyes. To Emily's relief, she didn't ask questions.

'It's a lonely life,' was all she said.

Yes, Emily knew the loneliness of singlehood all too well, but she was resigning herself to a life on her own. It seemed to be her destiny.

'Look at you,' she told her grandmother. 'All the years I've known you, you've lived alone and you've always been the happiest, most stable person I know.'

'I didn't live alone from choice.' Her grandmother looked at her with a wistful smile. 'I've missed Jim every day of these past thirty years.'

'I'm sorry.' Emily was instantly filled with remorse. 'Of course you have.'

Perhaps it was just as well that Jude returned

then and they finished that particular conversation.

Playing the gentleman to the hilt, he helped Granny Silver out of her chair. 'Now, where can I take you?' he asked.

'Granny needs to get to the station to catch the train, if that's not too much trouble.'

'My pleasure.'

Perhaps Emily shouldn't have been surprised that Jude accompanied her as she saw her grandmother off at the station. After all, he'd been at his most gallant from the moment he met Granny.

'I can see why you're so fond of her,' he told Emily as the carriage bearing the small white-haired figure in a lavender suit disappeared. 'She's charming.'

Emily nodded. 'She's always been super-understanding and ahead of her time, really. I think I valued her true worth when Alex came out. She was so sensitive and supportive.' She shot Jude a smile. 'You were a hit.'

'Talking of hits…' he said.

'Yes,' Emily said quickly. 'I'm sorry. I've been meaning to apologise for last night.'

'So have I, Emily. I didn't mean to deceive you, but I was worried that I might embarrass you if I tried to explain. It's not all that easy to tell a girl you've just met that you're not gay so she'd better watch out!'

'I might have hit you for that as well,' Emily admitted with a small smile. But at least the subject was out in the open now, and she felt much better as they headed back to the apartment.

Jude, on the other hand, was subdued again. To make matters worse, clouds had arrived to block out the sun and the city looked grey and depressing and cold. Emily tried to make light conversation. They squabbled mildly over the restaurant bill and Jude insisted that he didn't want to be reimbursed.

All the way home, however, she wondered about the problem that was troubling him. 'Are you sure you're OK?' she asked.

Jude's eyelids lowered as if he found her question tiresome. 'I'm fine, Emily,' he said in a bored tone, which made her feel like a fusspot rather than a concerned friend.

When they arrived at the apartment, he spoke almost sharply. 'Right. I need to get to work.'

Without another word, or the suggestion of a smile, he disappeared into his room, shutting the door firmly behind him.

Emily's feeling of rejection made no sense at all.

CHAPTER FOUR

JUDE let out a soft groan as he leant back against his closed door. He hoped Emily hadn't guessed that the pain had come back with a vengeance on the way home.

After a couple of calming breaths, he crossed his room, opened the drawer in his bedside table and snatched up the bottle of pills, downing two tablets swiftly, grimacing.

He sank onto the edge of his bed and felt the facade he'd worn all afternoon peel away. He'd enjoyed the company of Emily and her grandmother. In fact, he'd been somewhat stunned by how very much he'd enjoyed lunching with them. No doubt he'd been grateful for the diversion.

But now he allowed himself, for the first time since he'd left the doctor's office, to consider his fate.

There'd been good news and bad.

The doctor had been quite cheerful as he delivered the good news that a growth on Jude's pituitary gland was not malignant. Apparently these tumours were relatively common and could be removed by simple, but necessary, surgery via the nose. The gland was not secreting excess hormones, so Jude was lucky in that respect. The complications should be minimal.

Then had come the bad news—and even the doctor couldn't smile about the fact that the growth was pressing on Jude's optic nerve, meaning that he would go blind if he didn't have the operation. The surgeons would do everything possible to save his sight, but there was still a significant risk that the surgery might cause irreparable damage.

Significant risk. Bloody hell. Was that medico speak for *we don't like your chances, mate*?

Jude had challenged the doctor. 'Give me figures, man. What aren't you telling me? Do I have a fifty-fifty chance of blindness? Worse?'

The fact that the doctor wouldn't commit to a figure freaked the hell out of Jude.

Nausea rolled in his stomach now as he allowed himself, finally, to contemplate the full impact of going blind.

How could he possibly cope? Reading and writing were his life. He'd built his dream home in the mountains with spectacular views over the rainforest. His hobbies included observing the forest wildlife and hiking the rocky and difficult skyline. If he couldn't see, his life as he knew it would end.

Under the surgeon's knife.

Sure, there was Braille and there were talking books and voice activated software for his computer, but Jude's independent spirit ranted and rebelled at the thought of using them.

He hated the idea of being reliant on others for support or help. He couldn't bear it. Independence was in his blood and his bones. He'd learned it at his father's knee. He mustn't lose it. He mustn't.

And there was so much more to lose than mere self-sufficiency...

He would never again see the face of a beautiful woman like Emily. He would never savour that moment of opening a brand-new book and turning to the first page, seeing the shape of the words on the crisp white paper, encountering the magic of the first tempting sentence.

He would never watch a Broncos footy game, or see a sunset or the fresh perfection of an apple, would never see rain scudding across a city street.

Right now, he couldn't even be grateful for his imagination, which would continue to see these things even if his eyes could not. It was too soon to be thinking like flaming Pollyanna.

Yes, he knew he had to man up about this. He had to think positively and deal with whatever came his way, but for one afternoon he wanted to shut out the world. And, yeah, maybe feel more than a little sorry for himself.

The tablets had begun to ease the wretched ache that gripped his skull when he heard a gentle tap on his door.

At his grunted response, the door opened and Emily stuck her head through the gap, her sunset hair glowing like a candle flame in the twilight darkness of his room.

'Sorry. I thought you were working,' she said.

'Taking a break.'

Her expression suggested that she didn't believe him, and no doubt her deductions were aided by the fact that he was lying in the dark and hadn't opened his laptop.

'I've made a light supper,' she said. 'Scrambled eggs and toast, and a pot of tea.'

'Wonderful, thanks.'

'I'll put the tray on the desk here, shall I?' Emily spoke in the soothing tone of a nanny talking to a sick child. Having set the tray down, she stood in the middle of the room, twisting her hands nervously, as if she was waiting for him to explain what had happened.

He contemplated telling her the truth. He'd kept one truth from her already and she'd made it very clear that she hadn't appreciated the deception. But illness was different, surely? Why burden her with his personal worries when she had enough of her own?

'Is there anything else you'd like?' she asked at last.

'No, this is perfect. Thank you.'

With visible reluctance, she left him, closing the door behind her with a soft click. A few minutes later, he heard the TV come on in the living room—with a loud burst at first and then turned low. He imagined Emily eating her supper on her lap, watching the television alone, and he felt more depressed than ever.

When morning arrived, slanting sunlight through the blinds, Jude blinked awake and was relieved to discover that he was feeling fine. In fact, he felt so good it was hard to believe that he needed an operation in a week's time.

Seven days' grace.

He drew a deep breath. He wouldn't think beyond this week. Not yet. For now, he wanted to consider the best way to spend the precious time he had left.

A conscientious writer would tackle the ending of the book he was working on—get it finished and out of the way, in case there were any dreaded complications.

Jude shot a glance to his laptop, still lying closed on his desk. Normally, he looked forward to opening it each morning and starting work. Each new day gave him the chance to play creator and there were always surprises and fresh challenges, and occasional moments of deep satisfaction. As far as he was concerned, he had the best job in the world.

But now…

Everything was different this morning.

This next week could be his last week as a sighted man. He smashed that thought almost as soon as it arrived. He couldn't bear to think about trying to manage his writing career if he couldn't see.

Even so, he felt a burning compulsion to make the most of this week. He wanted to take time out to see all the things he loved one more—hopefully not for the last—time. Art galleries and museums, the botanical gardens, a ferry ride on the river. A day on Stradbroke Island. Lots of movies.

Books.

Girls…

Yeah…if only he could spend entire days sitting on a park bench watching beautiful women saunter by.

After showering and dressing, he took last night's supper tray to the kitchen and stashed the rinsed crockery in the dishwasher. Then he filled a mug with coffee from a freshly made pot that Emily had left on the bench and went in search of her. He needed to let her know that at least he was fine again. He found her on the balcony, drinking her coffee in a patch of sunlight.

Even when she was wearing a simple white blouse and jeans she looked lovely enough to cause a catch in his throat. Her face, when she saw him, was an instant picture of concern.

'I'm OK,' he told her before she could ask.

Her eyes narrowed in an assessing gaze that clearly said she thought he was lying. But Jude was determined to keep his health problems to himself. It would be bad enough when he had to ring his sister in Sydney to tell her his news.

'Just the same, I am taking a few days off,' he admitted, pulling out one of the balcony chairs and sitting with his legs stretched in front of him while he feasted his gaze on the Brisbane River as it sparkled in the morning sunlight. 'I need a few days away from the computer to give my eyes a rest. I thought I might do a bit of sight-seeing to refill the well.'

'What well?' Emily frowned in obvious puzzlement.

'The well of inspiration.' He shot her a smile. 'Finding fresh sights and experiences to keep the muse happy.'

'Oh, yes, I can see how that would help.' Emily looked as if she'd like to quiz him further, but she said instead, 'I'm sure food helps, too. What would you like for breakfast?'

'Emily, you don't have to keep feeding me.'

'I've told you I'm happy to.'

'I know you are.' He rose again, struck by a new restlessness. 'But if we're going to eat breakfast together, we might as well find a café down the street. Broaden our horizons.'

'OK. That sounds good.'

On a wave of generosity, Jude added, 'Afterwards, I'm going on a sightseeing jaunt. You're welcome to join me.'

This time Emily frowned. 'Jude, this isn't a date, is it?'

'Not at all,' he hurried to reassure her. 'I only asked because I know you're at a loose end.'

She didn't respond straight away. She seemed to be weighing up everything in her mind, and Jude was already wishing he'd done the same before jumping in with his rash invitation.

He'd been avoiding his friends because he didn't want them to discover his health problems and start offering sympathy. He should have been equally cautious with Emily. Then again, she'd witnessed two rounds of his headaches now without getting too nosy, and she *was* good company. And he *had* told Alex that he'd keep an eye on her.

On the plus side, if Emily accompanied him, he would be able to look at her as often and as long as he wanted to. Surely, given his future, getting an eyeful of Emily was the best justification of all.

'All right,' she announced, after frowning out at the view for several long seconds. 'I'll come but on one condition.'

'Ah, yes…your conditions.' Jude nodded. 'We still haven't discussed the terms of your truce, have we?'

'No, we haven't.' She eyed him sternly. 'Obviously, there'll be no more kissing, Jude.'

'Obviously,' he repeated dryly, even though the very thought of kissing her sent a jolt of desire firing low and hot. 'Is that all?'

'I'll keep you informed if I think of anything else.'

'So you're making up the rules as you go?'

'Absolutely.' Her serious expression morphed into an arch smile. 'A girl can't be too careful.'

Nor can a guy, Jude reminded himself.

There was method in her madness, Emily decided. She was worried that Jude was hiding something, that he hadn't told the truth about his trip to the hospital yesterday.

She hoped she was mistaken and that he was fine. It was almost impossible to imagine that such a vital man with the physique of an athlete could be unwell. But after two bouts of terrible headaches, there was clearly something wrong. If for no other reason, she should accompany him for his own good. If he had another bad spell while he was out, he might need her help.

By the end of the morning, she was pleased for other reasons that she'd come along with Jude. It was genuinely fun to visit the museum and the art galleries with such an interesting companion. Jude seemed to know so much, but he shared his knowledge in a way that was entertaining, without arrogance or obvious showing off.

One thing that surprised her was the way he sometimes stopped and just stared at things. It was predictable enough behaviour in art galleries or at the museum, but at other times his attention would be captured by the most unexpected things like branches of a winter-bare tree silhouetted against the noon sky. Sunlight slanting on an ancient carved church door. The sight of a striped deckchair on a rooftop.

Jude seemed to be soaking these scenes in.

He was stopping to stare again now as they walked through a stretch of parkland after a picnic lunch. A white heron was wading in the shallows of a pretty reed-fringed pond and Jude came to a halt to watch it, which might have been fine if his expression hadn't been so disturbingly sad.

Emily wanted to ask him if he was all right, but she knew that would probably annoy him. To distract herself from worrying, she decided that he was imagining a scene for his current story.

'Are you thinking that this bird might be

booby-trapped and that it's about to blow up?' she asked.

Jude blinked and looked at her strangely, as if he feared she'd lost her marbles.

'You were staring so hard, Jude. I thought the heron must be inspiring your imagination, and you were thinking up a scene for your book.'

He laughed. *Oh, wow.* He looked so amazingly handsome when he laughed.

'That hadn't occurred to me,' he said and his smiling gaze lingered on her. 'It's not a bad idea. But, as a bird-lover, I've a strict code of ethics. No birds are harmed during the writing of my books.'

Emily grinned. 'Then perhaps there's a beautiful woman trapped inside the body of a heron.'

This time she was rewarded by an extra gleam of appreciation in his eyes, a bright sparkle in the grey depths.

'You're the one with the fabulous imagination, Emily. Perhaps you should be making up stories, too.'

'Not a chance.' There were limits to her imagination.

'Perhaps the heron could be an alien sent to Earth to observe humans,' Jude suggested.

'Yes, or it might have a surveillance device attached.'

He stopped again. The tall white bird was standing on a flat shelf of rock in the middle of the pond. Tall and dignified, its feathers gleamed pure white.

'Or it might just be a beautiful bird fishing in the winter sunshine,' Jude said quietly. 'And we're mere humans admiring the perfect simplicity of nature.'

Something about the way he said this brought a lump to Emily's throat. She felt as if he'd shared an incredibly meaningful moment with her, and she had an absurd impulse to give him a hug, or to slip her arm through his and walk companionably close to his side.

Thank heavens she'd resisted the impulse. Not only would she have shocked Jude, she would have broken her new resolution to toughen up. For a moment there, she'd been carried away by her feelings. She'd felt a deep emotional connection with Jude. But feelings and emotions were highly dangerous. She'd learned the hard way that she couldn't trust them.

All her decisions from now on had to be made with her head, not her heart.

'So what happens first?' Jude asked much later, coming to stand beside Emily at the kitchen bench.

She'd offered to teach him how to cook a stir-fry, as a simple alternative to tinned soup.

This close, however, Emily could smell his aftershave. Fortunately, she resisted the temptation to lean in to the woodsy, masculine scent.

'First we cut the vegetables into thin, even strips.' She wished she felt calmer as she handed him a carrot. Jude, with a knife in one hand and a carrot in the other, looked more attractive than any man should in such a domesticated setting.

She turned her attention to her own chopping board and asked crisply, 'Why don't you tell me about the women in your life?' She needed a reality check. *Now.*

'Why would you want to know about them?'

'I've told you about my disastrous love life, so

it's only fair you spill about yours. Is there anyone special?'

Jude didn't answer at first, and Emily began to slice mushrooms with the care of an artist.

Standing beside her, Jude said, 'If I was seeing someone else I wouldn't have kissed you the other night.'

Her knife slipped, almost cutting her thumb. Memories of his kiss flooded her—the taste of his lips, the strength of his arms, the woozy, warm sensation that had flowered inside her.

'It's reassuring to hear that not every man is as sleazy as my two-timing ex,' she said tightly. 'By the way, you need the oil to be really hot before you add the meat.'

She added strips of grain-fed beef to the hot oil in the wok and began to stir them briskly. 'And on that other matter, I'm sure you've had a string of girlfriends, Jude.'

He stopped slicing a capsicum and stood watching her, eyes flashing unreadable sparks. 'Sure, we've established I like girls.'

Emily drew a sharp breath. 'Let me guess. But you're not the marrying kind.'

'That pretty much sums it up.'

'Do you have any special reason for dodging the altar?' Heavens, she couldn't believe she was being so nosy.

Jude's eyebrows lifted as he considered this. 'Perhaps I'm attracted to the wrong kind of girl.'

What a cop-out.

Her lips parted, ready to let fly with a smart retort, but her eyes met Jude's again. Locked in his grey gaze, she felt an unsettling tremor skip down her spine and her desire to be a smart mouth disappeared. Her heart beat strangely fast.

Dismayed by her reaction, she concentrated on adding onion and garlic to the wok. But as she recovered her wits, she felt compelled to ask, 'So what kind of girl is the wrong type for you?'

'You certainly like asking the hard questions.'

'I'm congenitally curious.'

Jude pursed his lips. His grey eyes shimmered. 'OK. My problem is I tend to go for professional women with an independent streak.'

Emily's jaw dropped. 'And that's a problem?'

'Sure.'

'What's wrong with women who are professional and independent?' She prided herself on having both these qualities. Not that her interests were relevant.

Jude was smiling now, as if he knew Emily was digging a very deep hole that she might very soon fall into. He reached for a stick of raw carrot from the pile he'd made. 'In theory, dating career women is fine. But I have a house at Mount Tamborine, and that's rather inconvenient for girlfriends with really important and demanding careers.'

'Such as?'

Good grief. She was asking *way* too many questions, but now she'd started she couldn't stop. It was like trying to stop eating a chocolate bar after just one bite.

Jude's raised eyebrows signalled his amused disbelief. 'You want a list of my girlfriends' careers? Well…let's see. There was Suze, who was an airline pilot, and Keira was an Army doctor, and Gina was a research scientist—'

'OK. I see what you mean,' Emily cut in, suddenly unwilling to listen to his entire list of lovers, even though she most certainly wasn't jealous. 'I guess I can see your problem. Women with those careers would appeal to a thriller writer, but they wouldn't suit a lifestyle tucked away in the mountains and far from a city.'

'That's it in a nutshell.'

Something in his voice made her look up. He was watching her with a mixture of amusement and thoughtfulness that sent her cheeks flaming.

Flustered, she tossed the sliced carrot and capsicum into the stir-fry and refrained from asking any more questions. After she'd added a generous dollop of sweet chilli sauce and stirred it through, their dinner was ready.

A girl with any sense would drop the questions, Emily told herself as they sat down. But she found her mind veering back like a boomerang to the subject of Jude's girlfriends. After her own problems with finding the right partner, she found Jude's apparent lack of success intriguing. He had everything going for him—brains *plus* looks. He was a great kisser, and he was even nice to grandmothers.

What was his fatal flaw?

'I know it's none of my business, Jude.'

'But you're going to ask anyway.'

'Do you mind?'

He shrugged. 'I become quite tolerant with food in my stomach. What do you want to know?'

'I was wondering if you've ever considered moving to the city to fit in with a girlfriend's career.'

It was some time before he spoke. 'I haven't given that serious thought,' he admitted at last. 'But I might, if I found the right girl.'

Emily thought how lucky that right girl would be.

'Then again,' Jude added, 'I might never find her. And who knows how any of us will feel in the future?'

Once again, she caught a shadowy flicker in his eyes. What was it that bothered him? She wished she could ask him about it, but she'd already asked far too many questions.

She drank some wine and said with a rueful smile, 'It seems we have something in common. I'm forever finding myself attracted to the wrong kind of man.'

Leaning back in his chair, Jude watched her through narrowed eyes. 'Have you worked out why?'

'If only I could. I'd give anything to understand why I choose men who'll hurt me.'

'Hurt you?' He looked shocked. 'But surely
that doesn't happen every time?'

'Too many times, I'm afraid.'

She sighed, and suddenly she found herself
needing to explain. Perhaps it was the relaxing
glass of wine, or perhaps she felt more comfortable with Jude now that he'd revealed something
about his own dating issues.

She found herself spilling the entire sorry
story of her relationship disasters, starting with
Dimitri in Melbourne and then Dave on the
rodeo circuit.

Surprisingly, Jude was very good at listening—every bit as good as Alex was. Emily went
on to tell him about her attempts to take control
of her dating.

'You know your problem, don't you?' said
Jude.

Unsure how to respond, she simply stared at
him.

His mouth quirked into a lopsided smile. 'You're
such a stunner, Emily, guys can't help themselves.
And on top of that, your job puts you in a posi-

tion of power, so you attract men with big egos who see you as a trophy.'

'So they didn't really care about *me*, just the way I looked?'

He shrugged his shoulders. 'It happens.'

Jude was probably right, Emily realised, thinking about Michael.

Oh, help. Michael.

For large chunks of today, she'd managed to push him out of her thoughts, but now she was remembering everything. The whole picture of their relationship unrolled in her mind like a tragic movie—the way he'd courted her so persuasively, the lavish gifts he'd bought for her, the late-night phone calls from Adelaide, the South Pacific holiday they'd planned together...

Then the Facebook page...

It was only when Jude reached across the table and squeezed her hand that Emily realised she'd been sitting silent for too long, a glum statue, wrapped in her unhappy memories.

Now, the pressure of Jude's strong, warm fingers wrapped around hers was incredibly comforting.

Perhaps it was a little too comforting. Without

warning, all the pain and emotion she'd been holding inside seemed to swell and burst up through her.

Her mouth pulled out of shape as she tried to explain. 'He said he loved me.' It was almost a wail. 'He *told* me he loved me.' Her voice broke on a choking sob.

And then, as if she'd cracked wide open, she began to weep without any hope of stopping.

In a heartbeat, Jude was out of his chair and beside her, wrapping his strong arms around her shaking shoulders.

'I'm s-s-sorry,' she spluttered against his neck.

'Don't be,' he murmured. 'You need to let it out.'

Then he was hugging her and she was out of her chair and clinging to him with her face pressed into his shirtfront, while his arms supported her and he murmured soothing noises into her hair.

It was some time before Emily's sobbing subsided and she was aware of Jude's fingers stroking the back of her neck…gently…so wonderfully gently. Beneath her cheek, his chest was a solid wall of strength, and she thought that being in his arms might very well be the most comforting sensation she'd ever experienced.

She couldn't remember ever weeping all over a man before. She'd always done her weeping after they'd left her.

Now, with some reluctance, but feeling strangely calmer, she lifted her head. 'Thank you,' she said softly, taking a step back out of Jude's embrace. 'I seem to be stretching your hosting duties way beyond reasonable bounds.'

'Emily, holding you in my arms is hardly a chore.'

For a moment she thought he was going to kiss her again. She certainly wouldn't slap him if he did, and when she looked into his eyes she saw a dark grey heat that suggested he knew this.

The air was practically crackling with electricity.

Surely that was dangerous.

They'd both agreed that another kiss mustn't happen. It would be like jumping from the fire back into the frying pan.

She gave a shaky laugh. 'Isn't a crying woman a man's worst nightmare?'

To her surprise, Jude touched her cheek and

wiped a damp tear track with the pad of his thumb. His eyes were serious as he smiled. 'You've been meeting the wrong men.'

'Well, yes, I think we've established that.'

She took a deep, necessary breath, grateful for his understanding, and especially grateful that neither of them had undermined this healing moment with another kissing mistake.

Why let attraction ruin a promising friendship?

'Thanks, Jude. I think it was cathartic to let that out. I must admit I feel much better.'

Quite miraculously better, Emily realised as they carried their dishes to the sink. She could think of Michael now without an accompanying surge of anger and shame. For the first time she could see him clearly for what he was—a silly, weak man who hadn't deserved her love, and who certainly didn't deserve his nice wife and family.

Thank heavens she'd been strong enough to tell him off and to send him packing. She was especially grateful that Michael was fully aware of her disdain for his behaviour.

She felt a new confidence now, a sense that in time she would be able to move on.

Much later, in bed, Emily thought about all of this again calmly. It was rather amazing that she'd come to Brisbane to seek comfort and understanding from Alex, only to receive it from a totally unexpected quarter—her cousin's temporary houseguest.

Jude was such a surprise package. A bit of a tall, dark, handsome mystery, really.

She thought again about the odd moments when she'd caught him looking worried, and she wondered if there was any way she could help, or whether, in fact, it was time for her to leave. She could go and visit Granny Silver for a bit. Perhaps she should suggest it to Jude in the morning?

She didn't want to outstay her welcome.

CHAPTER FIVE

EMILY wasn't given the chance to make this suggestion the next morning. Jude jumped the gun.

By the time she came into the kitchen he'd already made breakfast for both of them. A coffee pot was ready on the table, and there were bowls of pink grapefruit sprinkled with brown sugar, with boiled eggs and buttered toast to follow.

'I'm seriously impressed,' she told him. 'Seems you're a man with hidden talents.'

'Needs must,' he countered. 'I've decided to drive home to the mountains today. I have quite a few things to do there, so I wanted an early start.'

'Oh, right. Good idea.' Emily hoped she didn't sound as disappointed as she suddenly felt. Really, this reliance on Jude for company was a worrying trend. For heaven's sake, hadn't she been thinking of moving out today?

As if he'd sensed her disappointment and felt

responsible, Jude said, 'You could come with me if you like.'

Emily gulped on the piece of grapefruit she was eating, shocked by the leap of pleasure his suggestion triggered. Not only would she enjoy a drive into the mountains, but she was also curious about Jude's home. And the prospect of another full day in his company was very attractive.

That, however, was the danger.

The more time she spent with Jude, the more she liked him.

She was increasingly confused about her feelings, actually. After Michael, she'd been relieved to meet a man she could be friends with, without the threat of romance. Jude's kiss had been a stumbling block. He'd been on his best behaviour ever since then, yet she was still worried.

Yesterday, she and Jude had drawn quite a lot closer. She'd never experienced anything quite like that conversation in the park, watching the heron. Or the comfort of his hug when she'd had the Michael meltdown.

But there'd also been tummy-tingling thrills

that bothered her with mounting frequency, and this was a problem Emily couldn't ignore.

Apart from the slip with the kiss, Jude hadn't made any attempt to attract or seduce her, and yet she was plagued by a sense of building excitement whenever she was with him.

It was quite different from anything she'd experienced before.

She was quite sure that travelling to his mountain retreat would only add to her problems. It was a step too close. Too intimate. She should be pulling back from this man, not drawing closer.

Besides, Jude was probably just being polite with his belated invitation.

'I'm afraid I can't come,' she said carefully. 'I've already made plans for today.'

There was a flash in Jude's eyes that might have been disappointment, or relief.

But his response was cheerful enough. 'That's OK.'

Fortunately, he was too polite to ask what her plans for the day were. She would have been hard pressed to answer him. Perhaps he understood her wariness about getting too close. No doubt he shared her caution.

She wondered if she should mention her plan to leave, but he was keen to be on his way so she decided to leave it till his return.

'Don't hang about here, Jude. I can tidy the kitchen. I might give the apartment a once-over as well.'

'There's no need. I could never keep this apartment up to Alex's spotless standards so I've hired a woman to take care of it. Today's her day. She'll be here about nine.'

With a quick smile, he grabbed an apple for the road. 'I'll see you later then.'

It was the weirdest day for Emily. She knew it was madness to feel so fidgety and *lost* simply because Jude was away for the day. She'd been quite pleased with her idea to clean the apartment as a thank-you present, but if a cleaning woman was on her way there was no point. So, at a total loose end, she caught a bus into the city for a little retail therapy.

By mid-morning, however, she'd only bought another of Jude's books and a beautiful scarf for Granny Silver's birthday. After that, she wandered aimlessly up and down the Queen Street

Mall, unable to dredge any further interest in shopping.

In a coffee shop she ordered a latte and sat in a booth by a window, nursing her mug, savouring the coffee's smoothness and its soothing rich flavour. Staring out at the passing faces in the street, she allowed herself, for a fanciful moment, to imagine what it would be like to live with a writer, like Jude, in a secluded mountain hideaway.

Would she miss her job at the bank, or would she jump at the chance to follow her secret yearning to start her own online business?

Her happiness would depend on whether the writer in question had been honest with his feelings and truly loved her.

Whoa. Emily almost spilled her coffee. She couldn't believe she'd allowed her mind to wander into such crazy territory. It was so utterly pathetic.

Clearly, being on leave from work was not good for her.

When her phone rang with a friendly *quack*, she grabbed it from her bag, grateful for the distraction, although a part of her silly brain was instantly hoping that the call was from Jude.

It was from Alex.

'Hi, Emily.' His voice, coming all the way from Germany, sounded wonderfully clear and near. 'How are you?'

'I'm fine, thanks. How lovely to hear from you. How's Frankfurt?'

'Mad. Fascinating. Inspiring.'

'Sounds exciting.'

'It is. Listen, I'm ringing quickly between appointments to find out how Jude is. I could only get a cleaning woman at home.'

'Jude's fine. He's gone home to Mount Tamborine for the day.'

'Really? That's fantastic. So it's nothing serious?'

'Sorry, Alex. I don't know what you mean.' Tendrils of alarm snaked through Emily's insides. She gripped the phone so tightly she almost crushed it. 'What are you talking about?'

Jude stood on the deck at the back of his house, drawing deep lungfuls of fresh, sparkling air as he stared at the breathtaking view of lush rain-forest-covered mountains.

He was glad he'd come home. There'd been a risk of another headache attack on the winding roads, but he actually felt fine, and now he took a long soul-wrenching look at the place where he'd made his home. He never failed to be up-lifted by this majestic scenery.

There was something almost spiritual about its beauty. So much grandeur in the tumbling steepness of the hillsides. So many shades of green in the tree canopies and the undergrowth of lianas and ferns and palms. Even now, in the middle of the day, a wispy veil of white mist drifted around the tallest peaks.

At the thought that he might never see any of this beauty again he felt…*gutted.*

Gutted in the worst sense of the word. Empty. Bleeding.

Dead.

Hell.

What would you think of me now, Dad?

His father had always been so stoical about ill-ness. Jude would never forget the day his barrister dad collapsed after being away in Sydney all week for an important court case.

Quite late on a Friday evening, Max Marlowe had come into the living room, tossed his leather briefcase onto a chair, turned to the sideboard to pour a Scotch, then pitched forward onto the Oriental carpet. It turned out that he'd burst his appendix and nearly died.

Later, the family learned that Max had been in pain all week, but he wouldn't allow anything to interfere with winning his court case. He was damned if he'd complain about a bit of bellyache.

'Silly old fool,' Jude's mother had said.

Jude had searched her eyes for a glimmer of fondness, anything to counter her scoffing tone, and he'd been mortified when he hadn't found it.

A groan broke from him now. He knew it didn't really make sense but, more than ever now, it felt important to be as tough as his old man. He had to shake off his negative thinking.

Closing his eyes, he centred his thoughts on the sounds around him, focusing on each bird call that came to him. Some were delicate and bell-like, others sharp and strident—the calls of the whipbird, the catbird, the rifle bird and the

trillers…the overhead screech of a flight of rainbow lorikeets. And, way below in the valley, the
distant sound of a creek cascading over rocks.

He tried to take comfort from this… Even if
he couldn't see, he would still be able to hear.
All of this. Every musical note.

But somehow…

It wasn't enough…

Damn. He was being morbid again. No doubt,
he'd be in a better mood if Emily were here to
cheer him up.

At the thought of Emily, Jude's grip on the
railing tightened. Against reason, against his
best intentions, there was a very good chance he
was falling for her. Seemed crazy, really, that he
could feel this way on the strength of one brief
kiss.

Well…one kiss and several days of her company and of feeling at ease to a degree that was
quite extraordinary. Then again, perhaps he'd
simply been intoxicated—as had others before
him—by her smile and her dancing blue eyes
and the fiery silk of her hair.

It was a miracle that he hadn't kissed her again
last night. As he'd held her in his arms while

she wept over that lowlife ex, Jude had drawn on willpower he hadn't known he possessed. Which suggested that there was more going on than his physical need for her.

Emotions were involved.

A jagged sigh escaped him. He couldn't have chosen a worse time for emotional entanglement. There was no way it could work. Given Emily's history with men, she was sensibly avoiding new relationships, so even if he was totally well she wouldn't want to get involved.

Bottom line…he wasn't well, so the option for involvement wasn't even there.

Besides, with his lifestyle he had nothing to offer a career-focused bank manager. Which meant he was facing his old problem, with a whole new set of health problems on top of it.

The reality was—and here was the biggie— if he lost his sight he would not tie himself to any woman. He'd buy a tape recorder and the dreaded voice recognition software and he'd spend his days dictating his books into a machine.

The thought chilled him.

He loved writing, loved it with a passion that

he rarely admitted to anyone, and he'd fought hard to make this career his.

His parents had been dead against it. They were determined that he would study Law, but while Jude was fascinated by the cause and effects of crime, he had no desire to follow in his parents' footsteps.

No chance of happiness there.

Naturally, they believed he'd wasted his university years, studying Arts with no clear career path, and they'd given him little support during his years of hard slog and rejection while he was trying to find a publisher—writing long into the night and working as a newspaper reporter by day.

His satisfaction had come from loving his work, but could he still love it if he had to dictate his stories?

He hated the idea. He was a writer, not a speaker, and while some writers were also great oral storytellers, Jude knew he didn't share that talent.

Hell, how would he cope if the writing dried up?

Another chill crept over his skin like so many

spiders. Giving the railing an angry thump, he turned and went inside the house.

Later, in a calmer mood, he made a final tour of his home, taking mental snapshots of favourite items and rooms. He wondered if he should tell Emily, when he got back, about his impending operation. If she was going to stay on in Alex's apartment, it was only fair that she understood what was going on.

Perhaps he should suggest that she move somewhere else—to her grandmother's beach house maybe.

But when he imagined trying to tell her—trying to introduce the subject of hospitals and operations and the possibility of personal disaster—he recoiled from dumping all that doom and gloom on her when the poor girl was struggling with her own problems.

Why talk of hospitals and illness when all he really wanted was to make virile, wild, *healthy* love to her?

And, knowing what he did of Emily, she would probably feel involved in his problems. She would want to help him, to play nursemaid or hold his hand.

Hell. He would never want that. His masculine pride bucked and roared at the very thought.

Emily was on tenterhooks as she waited for Jude to come back that evening. She'd been totally rattled after Alex's phone call and his news that Jude was having medical tests for a potentially serious problem.

Obviously, Jude had avoided telling her the truth about his headaches. Which was fair enough—his health was his private business—but if he was in trouble, Emily wanted to help in any way she could.

She decided she needed to appear calm and unconcerned—Jude would hate any sign of fuss—so she'd gone to a fair amount of trouble to set the stage for his return.

Now, at six-thirty, he was due at any moment and she was dressed in a soft grey tunic over black leggings and sitting curled in an armchair, trying to look serene, with a book in her lap, although she was too keyed up to actually read it. She'd turned all the lamps on to show off the apartment at its gleaming, newly cleaned best, and she'd arranged a bunch of sunflowers in a tall vase on the coffee table to help the place to look extra cheerful. Upbeat mood music played softly.

Best of all, she'd found a wonderful recipe for Greek roast chicken and potatoes with masses of lemon and mustard and garlic, and now wonderful, tummy-tempting aromas wafted from the kitchen.

Emily thought she was waiting patiently enough, but when the phone rang her heart almost flew out of her chest. She jumped to her feet.

Calm down, she warned herself. It was probably just Alex ringing back, wanting an update on Jude, but she wouldn't have news until Jude arrived. She took a steadying breath as she picked up the receiver.

'Emily.' It was Jude's voice. 'How are you?'

'I...I'm fine.' Why was he telephoning? She'd been expecting him to walk through the door at any moment. 'Where are you?'

'I'm still at my place at Mount Tamborine. I'm afraid something's come up, and I need to stay on here for a few days to sort it out.'

A few days!

A flood of disappointment swamped Emily.
She'd been so on edge, so waiting for his return,
so anxious to have everything perfect for him.
He'd been incredibly understanding and kind
to her, and if he was in trouble she'd wanted to
return the favour.

Clearly, he had other ideas.

'Emily, are you there?'

'Yes.' She gave a little shake, trying to throw
off her disappointment. 'I'm sorry to hear that
something's come up. I hope you're all right,
Jude.'

'Yes, I'm fine.'

Yes, well, she now knew that this was a lie.
'You might need to ring Alex then,' she said a
shade too crisply. 'It would be good if you could
reassure him. He called here today because he's
worried about you.'

'Really? All right. I'll give him a call.'

'Jude, I'm worried, too,' she couldn't help adding. 'Alex said you were having medical tests to
find out what's causing your headaches.'

She thought she heard a sigh on the other end
of the line. 'I realise it's none of my business...'

'I don't want to bother you with that stuff,

Emily.' Jude said this firmly, as if to ward off any argument. 'You're on holiday and you should be having fun. Honestly, I'm OK. I have everything under control.'

She knew it was unreasonable to view this as another rejection. Jude wasn't a close friend. She couldn't expect him to confide in her or share his troubles, even though she'd done exactly that with him. But she didn't enjoy having her wonderful plans to support him come to nothing.

'Let me know if there's anything I can do to help,' she said glumly. 'Anything at all.'

'I will, Emily. If I need you, I'll be in touch. I have your mobile number, but hopefully you won't hear from me until it's all over.'

All over. That had to mean some kind of medical procedure, surely? An operation? Clearly, Jude was distancing himself from her, and Emily couldn't believe she felt so bad. It was ridiculous to feel rejected by Jude Marlowe when she'd only known him for…how long? Five? Six days?

She had to toughen up, had to show the grit that Jude's heroines had in spades. She cranked her features into a wobbly smile. 'You're certainly going to miss a darn good meal tonight,

Jude. Speaking of which, I'd better go. Don't want to let it burn.'

Then, because she had to, she added more gently, 'Take care, won't you?'

After she hung up, she went to the kitchen and turned the oven off, her enthusiasm for the new recipe having fizzled to nil.

Jude was tucking a water bottle into a side pocket in his backpack when he heard the sound of a car in his driveway. Crossing to the window, he scowled at the vehicle, a bright red sedan he didn't recognise. The last thing he wanted was to play host right now, when he was about to set out on a hiking trip.

From his vantage point, he had a clear view through the car's windscreen, and a familiar shimmer of red-gold made his heart thud. Hard. His throat constricted. What was Emily doing here?

He watched her climb out of the driver's seat and then lean in to haul out a cooler bag. She was wearing a longish grey top over black leggings and slim-fitting knee-high black leather boots.

She looked stunning, as if she'd just stepped off a plane from Milan or Paris.

Damn. Jude hadn't picked her for a busybody or, worse, a stalker. He wasn't sure he could handle this.

Her footsteps sounded on the stone path and he set his mouth into a grim scowl as he went to open the door.

'Hi, Jude.' Emily looked up from beneath long lashes and no doubt caught the surliness in his expression. Her face tightened. 'Before you get mad, Alex asked me to come to see you.'

Jude found this hard to believe. When he'd returned Alex's call, he'd instructed his agent to keep his condition confidential. He'd always believed that Alex was trustworthy, which was why he was one of the very few people Jude felt he could open up to.

'Alex kept his word to you,' Emily said next, as if she could read his mind. 'He hasn't told me anything he shouldn't have. I still have no idea what your problem is, and that's fair enough. I don't want to pry.'

Lifting her face, she met his gaze directly. 'But Alex is worried, Jude. He's very worried about you being up here on your own and…well…he asked me…actually, he more or less begged me to pop by, to check.'

Jude hadn't shifted from the doorway and Emily was still standing on the top step, fiddling with the strap of the cooler bag.

'As you can see, I'm perfectly fine.' He gave a bored shrug. 'I'm sorry, you've come all this way for nothing.'

Her blue eyes narrowed. Tipping her head slightly to one side, she regarded him with a surprisingly cool and measuring stare. Jude wondered if this was the look she gave her clients when they came to her bank, hoping to pull the wool over her eyes.

'Jude Marlowe,' she said in a quiet, no nonsense tone, 'you and I both know you're not fine. Alex believes your problem is quite serious, so forget the tough-guy act.'

Squaring her shoulders, she looked as serious as a hanging judge. 'Alex is your close friend and the poor fellow's stuck on the other side of the world, worried and helpless. Apart from that, it's only common sense that you shouldn't be alone. If you have one of your headaches, you'd be incapacitated up here.'

Jude flinched at the word *incapacitated*. 'I'm not that bad.'

Emily let out a noisy sigh. 'Why do you have to be so stubborn?'

He was certain she was about to deliver a lecture but, without warning, her face seemed to crumple and the hard glare in her eyes softened to concern. 'I'm worried about you, too,' she said in a small voice.

Jude struggled to resist. He'd been determined to keep Emily well clear of his troubles, although, in truth, he wanted nothing more than to haul her into his arms and to kiss her soft trembling mouth. Kiss her for a month. He'd been thinking of little else for days. Right now, he was imagining her long slim legs wrapped around his waist.

With a huge mental effort, he pushed his crazy desires where they belonged—clear out of his head.

But that still left him torn between two difficult choices. He could play the jerk and send Emily packing—or he could put himself through hell by inviting her into his home, *without* following through on his lustful urges.

He found himself apologising. 'I'm sorry. I don't want everyone worrying.' And then he took two steps back and stifled a sigh. 'You'd better come inside.'

'Thank you,' she said with dignity. She held up the cooler bag. 'By the way, I've brought you that chicken dinner you missed out on last night.'

Emily drew a deep, shaky breath as she followed Jude into his house.

Alex had warned her that Jude was fiercely independent and that she might have a battle on her hands. He was dead right. But she had to admit Jude didn't *look* as if there was anything badly wrong with him. He was as strong and sexy-looking as ever, and it was very easy to believe he was fine, especially here against the backdrop of his incredibly beautiful home.

He led her into a large open-plan area with acres of polished timber floors and massive uncurtained walls of glass that looked out into the rainforest. At one end of the space a sitting area held sleek leather couches grouped around an open fire.

The dining area was defined by a long Viking-style table, and beyond that the kitchen comprised solid timber benches and gleaming top-of-the-range stainless steel appliances.

Jude was certainly not a writer who starved in a garret, and he clearly had very good taste, or at least he'd employed someone with very good taste to design his home and to decorate its interior.

'This house is amazing,' Emily told him. 'It's absolutely gorgeous.'

'Thanks. I'm glad you like it.' He spoke politely and he was no longer scowling, but he wasn't quite his usual relaxed self. 'Can I make you a cuppa?' he asked, already heading for the kitchen.

'Only if you're having one. I hope I haven't interrupted anything important.'

He shook his head, not quite meeting her gaze, then turned on the kettle. 'Tea? Coffee?'

'I'll have tea, please. Do you mind if I take a look around?'

'Feel free.'

As Jude dropped teabags into mugs, Emily wandered. There were piles of books, magazines and newspapers scattered about the place, so it wasn't as tidy as Alex's apartment, and she guessed that Jude's freezer was stacked to the brim with frozen store-bought dinners, while his pantry would be crowded with tins of soup.

But, as a living space, his home had *wonderful* vibes. She loved all the natural timber and the huge walls of glass letting the forest in. It was like living in a tree house, looking out at the tall, straight trunks of massive trees, at fallen logs covered in moss and native orchids, and beautiful lush tree ferns.

This wonderful environment was also home to the birds Jude loved. Right now, Emily could see a flock of gloriously coloured rainbow lorikeets feeding on rainforest berries.

She stood, drinking in the beauty, thinking how creatively inspiring it must be for Jude to wake up each morning to this. Meeting him in the city, she would never have guessed…

'Here's your tea.'

She turned to find him standing behind her with their mugs.

'Thank you.' She sent him a smile as she took the red-and-white-striped mug he offered. 'I'm in awe, Jude. This is so beautiful, I feel like whispering, as if I'm in church.'

He smiled—for the first time, a proper, skin crinkling around his eyes smile. 'I know what you mean. It still gets me that way.'

As they headed for the sofas, her attention was caught by groupings of photos on a wall. A happy group shot of family or friends, a couple of beach holiday snaps, and another, obviously taken in an alpine region with people in bright-coloured mountaineering gear and parkas standing around several international flags.

'I can pick you out easily, in all of them,' she said.

Jude looked a bit younger and leaner and more suntanned, but it was impossible to mistake his dark hair, broad shoulders and arresting smile. In the alpine shot, he had his arm looped around the shoulders of an attractive athletic-looking woman with long dark hair.

'Are you a mountain climber?' Emily asked.

'Strictly an amateur, but I've climbed quite a few interesting peaks around the world.'

She bit down on her lip to stop herself from asking about the girl, who was none of her business.

About to turn away from the photos, her attention was caught by a framed photo of a young couple smiling and posing with what looked, from the equipment, like a rescue team. Again, Jude was included and there was a printed caption beneath the photo.

To our rescuers...we will never forget...from Tim and Jill Martin.

Emily blinked in surprise. 'So you not only climb mountains, but you're a rescuer as well.'

Wow. She was looking at Jude and his house with new eyes, which was possibly why, when she glanced back to the kitchen, she now noticed a backpack on the floor, propped against a cupboard. And then she realised Jude was wearing hiking boots.

'You don't have to stand about,' he said, waving his mug of tea towards the sofas. 'Come and sit down.'

Frowning, Emily disregarded the invitation.

'Were you about to set off now? Up the mountain?'

He shrugged and looked away. 'It's no big deal.'

'But were you?' she persisted. 'You've got your backpack ready and you're wearing boots. Were you planning to hike?'

He looked down at the mug cradled in his big hands. 'I was about to head off to Sunset Ridge. It's something I'd like to do before—' his throat rippled '—before I go into hospital.'

Emily gulped as she heard the word *hospital*. A hundred questions clamoured to be answered but she pushed them down. He would tell her if and when he wanted to.

'So the walk is really important to you?' she suggested.

Instead of answering her directly, Jude pointed to the view through one of the huge picture windows. 'See that ridge up there?'

Emily looked up to the outline of the mountains, solid and dark against the pale afternoon sky.

'Best view of the sunset you'll ever see is from up there,' Jude said quietly. 'One of the main reasons I bought this land is because it's the closest freehold to that ridge.'

'I guess that answers my question.' Following his gaze, Emily gave a slow nod. 'This walk is definitely important to you.' Her sideways glance met Jude's. 'But is it wise to go up there on your own?'

He was staring at her now, his grey eyes faintly amused and yet also challenging. 'Are you offering to join me?'

A pulse beat at the base of her throat. 'Are you inviting me to join you?'

'I guess I am,' he said with a slow, cautious smile.

CHAPTER SIX

EMILY'S first reaction to Jude's invitation was excitement, but she had to be practical. 'We wouldn't get back till dark, would we?' She was returning to Brisbane tonight, and she didn't like the idea of having to drive back down the unfamiliar mountain road in the dark.

'You'd need to stay the night, of course,' Jude said deadpan.

Talk about a turnaround. Five minutes earlier, he'd been determined to throw her out. Now, a cautious, untrusting voice whispered a warning to Emily. She found Jude far too attractive for her own good. Now, in this setting, he was more attractive than ever.

Problem was, she'd promised Alex she would keep an eye on him. How could she let him go traipsing up a mountain alone?

'I brought a pair of jeans and a sweater with me, but I don't think I have any suitable shoes,' she told him. She also wasn't sure she'd be able to keep up with an experienced mountain climber.

Jude ran an assessing gaze over her fashionable boots. 'I might have walking boots that'll fit you.'

'From an old girlfriend?'

His response was a slow tilted smile. 'Yes. The Army doctor, Keira, comes up here sometimes when she's on leave, but she wouldn't mind if you borrowed her shoes.'

Emily couldn't help feeling curious about what appeared to be an ongoing relationship with this former girlfriend. Not that it was any of her business.

They finished their tea, and then went downstairs to the garage where a couple of mountain bikes were stacked against a wall and a large green canoe was suspended from the roof. Jude opened a side door to reveal shelves stacked with backpacks, coiled ropes and other camping and outdoor gear. There was also a pair of women's hiking boots, which he handed to Emily.

'Try these, Cinderella.'

Conscious that he was watching her every movement, she sat on the stairs, took off her black boots and tried on the ones belonging to his girlfriend.

She reserved judgement until she'd tied up the laces and was standing, wriggling her toes. 'They feel fine.' She took a few steps. 'They're a good fit, actually.'

She sent him a surprised smile and Jude smiled back. It was their first shared smile since she'd arrived and it made her feel much happier than it should have.

But then she remembered the boots' owner. Obviously, Jude and this Keira were still quite close, and for a fanciful moment Emily imagined the boots were beginning to pinch her.

But they were fine, really, an uncannily good fit—and the hike wasn't long or particularly demanding. Although it was rather dark inside the rainforest and there was the occasional slippery patch on the track, the undergrowth wasn't thick, so, apart from dodging buttress roots and the occasional wait-a-while vine, it was fairly easy-going.

Jude made it look easy, of course, and Emily suspected that he'd slowed down for her. If there was a rocky creek to be crossed, or a mossy log to clamber over, he was always ready with a strong hand to help her. She wished she didn't enjoy those brief moments of contact quite so much.

Even discounting the pleasure of Jude's company, she genuinely enjoyed the hike. As a former dancer, she was fit and she loved any form of physical exercise that didn't involve throwing or catching a ball. And who didn't love a rainforest? Beauty abounded every step of the way, and always in the background there was the music of endless bird calls. Looking up, she was rewarded by bright glimpses of blue sky or golden sunlight streaming through the dense green canopy.

As they neared the top, the thick forest gradually opened out into sparser eucalypt trees, and then finally they were on a ridge.

Emily stood, breathing in the pure, clean mountain air. She opened her mouth to speak, but then she changed her mind as she realised that *wow* was totally inadequate. In fact, there wasn't any word she could think of that would do justice to this spectacular view to the west, with descending mountains and ridges as far as the eye could see.

After a bit, she said simply, 'Thanks for letting me come, Jude.'

He smiled, and there was a heart-stopping softness in his eyes that made her feel, in that moment, that they might have been the only two people on the planet.

'There's a seat along here.' His voice brought her back to earth and she followed him along the ridge till they reached a shelf of rock.

Indeed it made a very comfortable seat, smooth and warmed by the sun, with another smooth rock wall behind it forming a backrest.

'Definitely dress-circle seats for a sunset,' she said, looking out at the sky, already growing pink in the west, while a pair of huge wedge-tailed eagles circled and rolled on the air currents above the valley.

Jude handed her a water bottle and they sat quenching their thirst and taking in the spectacle. Emily asked him about his climbing experiences and he told her about his skyliner friends—fellow bush-walkers who added an extra challenge to their hiking by not sticking to the easy routes.

'We follow the tops of the ridges,' he explained. 'Any obstacles like gorges and fast-running mountain streams or cliff faces are simply part of the fun.'

She thought it was a very fitting activity for a somewhat reclusive thriller writer. The more she discovered about Jude, the more she was fascinated by him, and she was surprised that at least one of his former girlfriends hadn't been tempted into adjusting her lifestyle to blend more easily with his.

Or hadn't that been an option?

Then she forgot about his social life as the sun began to bleed liquid colour across the western sky. They stopped talking and simply watched in hushed awe as the heavens were stained with pink and orange deepening to crimson, and clouds were rimmed with bright shimmering gold.

It was so beautiful, they watched until the light began to fade. Emily stole a glance in Jude's direction, wondering if they should leave before it got too dark. Then she saw how unbearably sad he looked.

It was the same lost look she'd seen when he was watching the heron.

Perhaps worse. Such a depth of despair that she was shocked to the soles of her borrowed boots.

She wasn't sure if he was in pain again, or if he was worrying about his future. And then— oh, God—she almost fell off the rock as a worse thought struck. Had the doctors given him really terrible news?

'Jude,' she said softly. 'Are you OK?'

He blinked and the sadness evaporated. 'I'm fine,' he said. 'Why?'

'You were looking a bit grim.' She tried to make her voice light.

He sighed, then let out a soft chuckle. 'One way or another, you're going to get it out of me, aren't you?'

'Only if you really want to tell me.' She hugged her knees. 'I know we only met a week ago, but I think we've become pretty good friends in that short time. I know you've really helped me, and I'd like to think that I could be there for you, if you needed a friend.'

His gaze was fixed on the water bottle he was holding. 'I do appreciate your concern, Emily.' He continued to stare at the bottle, then he closed its lid with an emphatic snap, and took a deep breath as if he'd made a decision.

'I have to have an operation,' he told her flatly. 'There's a benign tumour pressing on my optic nerve, so there's a chance that I may lose my sight.'

No.

Oh, God, no.

Never in her wildest dreams had Emily imagined anything this awful.

Her throat was choked by a knot of pain. Her eyes stung. She wanted to cry—except that crying was the very worst thing she could do in front of Jude. He'd probably held back from telling her because he didn't want a sobfest making everything worse.

Jude…might go blind.

How truly frightening for him.

Suddenly, the more puzzling aspects of his recent behaviour began to make sense—the trips to the art galleries, and those unexpected moments when he'd stopped and simply stared at a tree or a bird—and now, at this sunset.

He'd been trying to capture those images, to hold them in his memory. All this time he'd been dealing with the terrifying prospect of blindness, and yet he'd said nothing to her. Instead, he'd listened to *her* silly problems with an ex-boyfriend and offered her comfort.

Oh, Jude...

Emily had never felt such a storm of emotions. Her desire to be careful was drowned by the overwhelming force of her feelings. All of which centred on Jude. Feelings deep and profound, and more genuine than anything she'd felt before.

She wanted to take him into her arms, to hold him against her heart. Wanted to be with him. For him. In any way he wanted.

Gulping back her tears, she slipped an arm around his shoulders. 'I'm sure there's a very good chance that everything will be fine.'

'Yeah. I'm thinking positively.' He gave her hand a squeeze. 'But this will get you into trouble.'

'Trouble?'

'Or it will get *me* into trouble.' He slanted her a smile. 'Just warning you. If you stay this close, I'll end up kissing you.'

Emily felt a jolt so strong she almost flew off the mountaintop. In this setting…with the sunset and the emotional wallop of his sad news… a kiss had never felt more necessary.

'If you do kiss me, I promise not to hit you.'

To her relief, Jude didn't stop to ask for further clarification. He gathered her in and the next moment they were kissing. They simply flowed together, as if their bodies had minds of their own. As if this was meant to happen.

She'd never known a kiss quite like it, hadn't known a kiss could be so moving. So sad. So blistering and sweet and healing. So full of heart and soul. Earthy, and filled with hungry need. She wound her arms around Jude's neck, needing to press closer, craving contact with every inch of him. Her insides caught fire, and she might have burned to ashes in his arms.

He suddenly went very still.

She heard him draw a deep shuddering breath.

'Oh, God, Emily.' He was breathing rapidly. 'This is crazy. I'm so sorry.'

'I'm not.'

'Emily.' Her name was uttered softly—half rebuke, half prayer.

'Don't start talking about mistakes, Jude. It was an emotional moment.' *Life-changing.*

'No doubt about that.' He touched her cheek just once, then pulled his hand away quickly. 'But this is my problem. You mustn't get too involved.'

Too late. I'm involved. So deeply it's scary.

Already Jude was reaching for the backpack, and his face was hidden in the gathering darkness. 'There's always going to be temptation when a man and a woman are alone, but this is the very worst time for either of us to get involved.'

So sensible. Now he sounded like a parent.

Worse…he was right. He was about to undergo surgery, touch-and-go surgery with potentially disastrous results. And Emily had made so many mistakes with men she ought to know better. She certainly shouldn't have made a rule about no kissing and then promptly broken it.

But wasn't this also a time when Jude really needed a caring and loving someone in his life?

'I hope you'll at least allow me to be a friend,' she said, flashing a brave smile. 'If nothing else, I could be Alex's stand-in.'

He looked at her for the longest time, as if he was giving this serious thought. But all he said was, 'We should be getting back.'

True. It was getting darker and colder by the minute, and this was neither the time nor the place to try to persuade Jude that he needed her, especially when she'd come to the mountains uninvited and invaded his privacy.

'Will we be able to find our way back to the house in the dark?'

'Sure.' From his pack, Jude produced little torches for them to strap around their heads, rather like miners' lights. As they set off, the narrow beams proved wonderfully effective, leaving their hands free to push vines out of the way, or for Jude to take Emily's hand to help her over rough bits, which he needed to do frequently.

The constant contact didn't help her to calm down.

It was quite cold by the time they reached the house and Jude was pleased to hurry inside and busy himself with lighting the fire, while Emily reheated her chicken dish. In no time the flames were crackling in the grate and the rich aroma of lemon-infused chicken and potatoes was wafting from the oven.

Jude drew the curtains, making the dark forest retreat, and the house became warm and cosy. And intimate. Dangerously so.

Obviously he had very poor self-control when Emily was around. The merest glimpse of her set his heart leaping. He wanted to stare and stare at her. To touch. And to taste her. Wanted to lose himself in her.

He'd almost kissed her senseless on the mountain this evening. It was a miracle he'd found the strength to pull back. If only he hadn't weakened and invited her to stay here overnight. They needed the no kissing rule more than ever now.

He didn't want his name added to the list of men who'd hurt her.

Apart from enjoying the Greek chicken, Jude seemed rather distracted. After dinner, when he and Emily sat on the sofa in front of the fire, he was careful to keep his distance.

And a very good thing, too. Emily knew she'd been carried away by the sunset and the flood of emotions that had come with hearing Jude's diagnosis. Now that she was calmer, she knew he'd been sensible to re-establish their boundaries. Friendships were so much clearer and safer than romantic entanglements.

If they stuck to friendship, hearts wouldn't be broken, lives wouldn't be turned upside down and everyone would remain happy. It was actually a relief to have this sorted in her head.

It left her free to concentrate on practical considerations, like Jude's impending trip to hospital.

'Who's going to look after you, after you leave hospital?' she asked him now. 'Do you have family you can call on? Are your parents still alive?'

'My folks were both killed in a plane crash in China ten years ago.'

'Gosh. How awful.'

'It was terrible,' Jude agreed. 'But in some ways I think my father wouldn't have minded going quickly like that. He couldn't stand being ill. Saw it as a character flaw. I know he would have hated growing weak or decrepit with old age.'

A log on the fire made a loud popping sound, and Emily watched a little spray of sparks as she digested what Jude had just told her. Perhaps his father's attitude explained why Jude was so stoical about his condition.

'Is there anyone else in your family?'

'My sister, Charlotte, in Sydney.' As soon as he mentioned her name his face softened. 'I've told her what's happening, of course, and she wants to help, but she has three young children, so I don't think she'll be able to get away for long.'

'So you—'

'I have plenty of friends. But I don't expect I'll need help. I'm sure I'll be fine.'

'It's such a pity Alex is away. He's never happier than when he's looking after someone.'

Jude smiled. 'That's why he's such a great agent.'

'You'll let me help, won't you?'

His smile faded. 'I'd rather you didn't.'

'Why?' It was impossible to keep the hurt from her voice.

'I'd rather get through this on my own.'

She bit down hard on her lip to stop herself from pleading. After all, a girl had her pride.

Quickly, she changed the subject. 'This must be the worst part—waiting for it all to be over.'

'If Alex had his way, I would have kept busy working—writing right up until they wheeled me into Theatre.'

She sent an eye-rolling smile towards the ceiling. 'This is one occasion where I can't agree with Alex.'

'So how do you think I should be spending my time?'

'Doing exactly what you've been doing. Seeking out your favourite sights, storing up memories.'

Jude's eyes widened. 'You've seen through my scheme?'

'Well…I assume you've been taking another look at your favourite things, like the art galleries and that heron in the park, and the sunset.' She hurried to add, 'Not that I think you'll need the memories, Jude. I'm sure you're going to be fine, but it's like having—' She paused, hunting for words.

'An insurance policy?'

'Exactly. Or backup for your computer.'

She wondered if Jude had included pretty women on his list of favourite things. But it wasn't a question she could ask, especially now, when his smile morphed into thin-lipped grimness and he kept his gaze fixed on the fire.

At midnight, Jude lay alone in the dark with his eyes closed, thinking about Emily.

Emily, Emily, Emily...

She was becoming a dangerous obsession.

He let his mind drift back to the first time he'd seen her when he'd opened the door to Alex's apartment and he'd found her standing there, dressed in her lovely white coat and long, sexy boots. Her bright red hair had tumbled about her shoulders like a fiery river and her blue eyes had sparkled and he'd forgotten how to breathe.

Her loveliness eclipsed any masterpiece in an art gallery, was more exciting than any magnificent sunset. And this evening when he'd kissed her he'd been consumed by disastrous longing.

Now, the longing wouldn't leave him. Emily was lying in another room, mere metres away, and he was torturing himself with fantasies of going to her.

He couldn't.

He mustn't.

He had too many freaking question marks hanging over his future.

They drove back to Brisbane in separate vehicles. Emily had offered to drive Jude in her hire care because she was worried he might develop a headache on the way down the mountain, but he'd politely refused and she knew she'd offended his masculine pride. She played the radio the whole way to distract herself from worrying.

As soon as they were back at the apartment, he promptly told her he was heading out. 'Just grabbing a few things for the hospital stay,' he called over his shoulder.

'Don't forget to put pyjamas on your shopping list.'

He turned back to her. 'Pyjamas?'

'Sleepwear, Jude. A two-piece garment. Top and bottom, usually matching.'

'Why are you suddenly worried about my sleepwear?'

His amused and glittering gaze held her trapped, and she had to swallow before she could answer.

'I'm not normally interested in what you wear to bed.' *Liar.* 'But I thought your holey T-shirts might frighten the nurses.'

He responded with a huffing sigh. 'Of course. Thanks for reminding me.'

After Jude had gone, Emily rang Granny Silver. She just had to talk to someone, and she knew her grandmother wasn't a gossip.

'Darling,' her granny soothed. 'I'm so sorry to hear such bad news, but the doctors are so clever these days. I'm sure Jude will be fine.'

'I know. I keep telling myself that. I just wish I was like you or Alex. You're so good at helping people in difficult times.'

There was an unexpected chuckle on the end of the line.

'What's so funny?'

'I'm sure Jude would much rather have your company, than either mine or Alex's.'

'I've already told you, Granny. Jude and I are just friends. Quite new friends at that.' Emily had been working hard to remind herself of this, and it helped to say it out loud.

'Well, yes…I'm sure that's sensible, Emily, given everything that Jude has ahead of him.'

'But I feel so helpless. I wish I could think of wise and comforting things to say, or really practical ways to help.'

'You worry too much, dear. You have oodles of empathy. You put it into practice every day in your work. That's why you make such sound decisions for your clients. You just need to put yourself in Jude's shoes. Follow your instincts and I'm sure you'll work out the best way to keep his spirits up.'

'All right. Thanks. Follow my instincts. I'll hold that thought.'

CHAPTER SEVEN

FOR Jude's last night at home he invited Emily
to join him at one of Brisbane's classiest restaurants.

This didn't surprise her as much as it would
have a week ago. She and Jude had spent a great
deal of time together in the past few days and
she couldn't help feeling secretly pleased that he
sought her company, even though many of his
friends had rung him after they'd received urgent but cryptic messages from Alex.

It appeared, however, that Jude was more comfortable spending time with a relative stranger
during these pre-surgery days than with old
friends. He seemed to hate having to discuss
his illness with these people when they rang.

Emily wasn't quite sure what to make of this.
She guessed that Jude saw illness as a weakness,
just as his father had. He would rather hide than
accept people's sympathy. So he was happy just

to spend time with her, no doubt because she was already in the know and didn't need to ask more questions.

Together, they'd spent a day on Stradbroke Island and they'd stood on Point Lookout, watching whales frolic; they'd been to a couple of movies, spent an afternoon scouring Alex's bookshelves and reading sections of books aloud to each other, spent a rainy afternoon making an elaborately layered lasagne.

There'd been no more kissing, which Emily knew was wise, given what loomed ahead for Jude. But they'd become quite close in an amazingly short time. There was something very *simpatico* about their tastes. If Emily ignored the silly tugs of longing that kept getting in the way, she very much enjoyed just being Jude's friend.

Tonight, however, she was very tense. She particularly wanted this final hospital-eve to be special. Hoping to look her best, she'd bought a very expensive dress in deep-chocolate silk.

'Good heavens,' Jude said when he saw her. 'Now *that* is a sight for sore eyes.'

Emily almost cried. 'How can you joke about it?'

'I'm not joking,' he said with a dry smile. 'The dress is gorgeous.'

Just the same, his half-joking comment about sights for sore eyes lit a tiny light-bulb idea. All week, she'd been thinking about her grandmother's comment. *You just need to put yourself in Jude's shoes.* Emily had been trying to think of a really unique and fun surprise that he'd like.

No, I couldn't. I couldn't possibly.

Just the same, a daunting but intriguing idea simmered at the back of her thoughts while they took their time over their delicious three-course meal, savouring the food and never once talking about hospitals or illness. Or relationships.

It was surprising how many other topics they could find—Jude's theories about space travel, Emily's thoughts on the global financial crisis, his ideas for future books, her dream of an online retail business.

Throughout the meal, Jude hardly noticed the restaurant's famous view of the city's lights. He was too busy watching the subtle play of lamplight on Emily's face, or watching her lips as she talked and the expressive way she used her slim, pale hands to elaborate a point.

He watched her hair and wished he could study it more intimately. He needed to understand how the red and gold blended. Were some strands darker than others?

So many things he needed to know...about Emily...

He longed to feast his eyes, and yes...to touch and to taste her. Wanted to rediscover the magic they'd started on the mountain. That one kiss had been so tantalising. He hadn't been able to get it out of his head, and there were times when he thought he might go mad from holding back. But sex with Emily was out of the question.

He knew that. A thousand times he'd told himself that he was grateful she'd been the perfect companion this week—warm with her smiles, ready with her wit, careful to keep her distance.

But he felt as if he was wasting precious time. He'd wasted days and nights in Emily's company, holding back while every cell in his body screamed at him to make sweet, wild love to her.

And now the hours were slipping away.

Soon there would only be minutes left.

Of course, despite their leisurely dining, the evening flew all too quickly. In no time they were back in the apartment, where the only sane action for Jude to take was to head straight to his bed. Alone.

'Thanks for your company.' He spoke with necessary formality. 'It was…fun.'

Fun was such an inadequate way to describe the depth of his pleasure in Emily's company. Given the circumstances, it was the best he could come up with.

He longed to close the gap between them. *Just one night, Emily.*

He turned to leave.

'Hey, hang on a sec,' she called after him. 'I want you to see something.'

Jude turned. 'What is it?'

'Put some music on,' she said enigmatically. 'Something with a good slow beat.'

'Why?'

'You're asking too many questions. Just take a seat and I'll be back in a moment.' Already she was off, down the hallway to her room.

Intrigued, he obeyed. He found a CD with a slow, sultry beat and he chose an armchair by the door and sat casually, with an ankle propped on a knee, tapping his fingers to the music as he waited.

And waited…

'Hello,' he called after five bemused minutes. 'What's going on? How long is this going to take?'

'Not much longer. Sorry. Coming soon.'

He wondered if Emily had lost whatever she'd planned to show him, but hell, he had nothing better to do. He waited a little longer. Told himself that no, he couldn't go to her room. That was madness.

He was about to call again when he caught a movement—a brief flicker of a shadow on the wall at the end of the hallway.

A sixth sense made his heart thud.

He dropped his relaxed pose and was instantly tense with anticipation.

And then…a leg appeared…a slim and shapely leg, spellbinding in sheer black stockings and black patent high heels.

Jude's jaw dropped so hard he was sure it must have dislocated. Transfixed, he watched as Emily gave a little dancer's kick and stepped into the room in a slinky short coppery silk dress.

The fabric was the colour of her hair and it hugged her curves divinely. Little black buttons ran down the front. Buttons and loops...

His heart began to thunder. What was going on? He couldn't believe this, but he sure as hell hoped it wouldn't stop.

A double bass pulsed, slow and sexy and deep.

A soft blush warmed Emily's cheeks and she smiled shyly and began to move forward in a smooth, hip-swaying dance, before kicking off one shoe...

And then the other...

Surely not?

Jude's blood pounded as Emily's hands fluttered to the hem of her dress. Then she pushed the silk aside, undid a suspender belt and began to peel down a stocking to reveal smooth pale skin that gleamed softly in the lamplight.

He couldn't believe it. Far out, she was going to strip...

It was quite possible that he'd stopped breathing.

Emily, for heaven's sake...you crazy, gorgeous girl.

She looked so beautiful, so desirable...but vulnerable, too.

Yes, vulnerable and brave, as if, deep down, she was scared...

And suddenly Jude got it. He guessed why she was doing this... He was almost certain that she wasn't aiming for seduction. This was a gift to add to his repertoire of memories.

Oh, Emily.

Couldn't she tell this was killing him?

But he couldn't have stopped her now even if he'd wanted to, which he didn't. He was nailed to the chair. Electrified.

She began to undo the buttons at the neckline of her dress. Slowly, with a grave little smile directed at a spot on the wall above his head. With the tiniest fumble of fingers on slippery silk... one button popped open to reveal a tempting glimpse of soft pale skin...

Somehow, Jude bit back a groan.

She performed a neat pirouette, and then she was facing him again, releasing a second button. Her dance continued—a sensual sway here, a bobbing kick there, and more buttons popped.

Three...

Four...

The copper silk fell away to reveal the creamy tops of her rounded breasts. Through delicate skin-toned lace, he could see their pink tips.

He rose out of his chair, his body on fire. She was so gut-wrenchingly beautiful...even lovelier than he'd imagined.

But his throat felt as if he'd swallowed shards of glass. He knew that beneath Emily's saucy bravado she was still...

Scared...

He wanted to tell her that she didn't have to do this, but he couldn't get the words past the sharp ache in his throat.

Tense as a bow string, he dragged in deep breaths. Then he realised that Emily had stopped dancing.

She was standing absolutely still in the middle of the room, watching him with round, worried eyes...

Then she flushed deeply and looked away, grabbing at the silken halves of her dress and pulling them over her lace-covered breasts. 'I'm so sorry.'

Hell.

'Don't be.' Jude forced the words past the burning logjam in his throat.

Emily was shaking her head, keeping her eyes averted. 'I…I've never done anything like this before. I don't know why I thought it was a good idea.'

'It's a fabulous idea, Emily. Amazing. Best idea you've ever had…'

'It was supposed to be a bit of fun, Jude. But…' Her lips trembled. 'But you looked so sad.'

'Did I?' Distraught, Jude stepped closer, touched a trembling hand to her chin and turned her face towards him. Tears glittered in her eyes.

He wanted to kiss the tears away, wanted to kiss her all over—the lobe of her ear, the palms of her hands, the hollows behind her knees, her pink-and-white breasts, wanted his lips on every sweet inch of her. Wanted to carry her to his room and stay there with her till the end of next summer…

But Emily was turning her back to him, and already she'd begun to do up her buttons. 'It was a stupid idea.' Her voice was high and tight. 'You probably think I'm a brazen hussy and that it's no wonder I can't keep a boyfriend for long.'

No, damn it. Now his eyes were stinging as well as his throat. 'Believe me, Emily, that thought did not cross my mind.' He spoke quietly, trying to calm her. 'I'm only thinking how beautiful you are—and how thoughtful.'

Just in time, he stopped himself from adding—*and how badly I want you.* 'I think I know why you did this.'

Her head jerked up and she stared at him in surprise.

'I'm guessing you thought this might be my last chance to see a beautiful woman…taking her clothes off.'

For a moment she continued to stare at him, then she looked away and her face crumpled. 'I'm sorry. I was trying to imagine what a man might want, but it was silly. I don't know why I thought it was a good idea.'

'Emily.' There was a rough tremor in his voice. 'It's a *great* idea. The best idea in history. Greater than discovering the wheel, or that the Earth is round, or putting beer into cans.'

She smiled weakly.

'My only complaint is that you stopped.'

Standing before him, looking utterly delightful as she clutched at her dress to protect her modesty, she stared at him, her mouth a perfect circle of surprise.

Perhaps she was coming to terms with what he was telling her. Eventually, the worry in her eyes lightened. 'So I should have kept going? I couldn't get that right, either?'

A strangled laugh broke from Jude as tenderness and desire waged war with his reasoning and common sense. 'I think I may be the one who's made the biggest mistake.'

'You?'

'For reinstating that crazy kissing ban.'

'Oh.' The word bounced softly into the space between them. Still clutching at her dress, Emily frowned. 'But this was meant to be purely for fun. I wasn't trying to—' She blushed. 'You don't want more complications in your life.'

'That's true,' he agreed reluctantly. 'And I don't want to mess up *your* life, either.'

He took a step closer, knowing it wasn't wise, and Emily seemed to melt towards him. Their fingers brushed and he was zapped by fire. He heard her soft gasp.

'I'd rather not risk joining the list of males who've hurt you,' he said.

She shook her head. 'Maybe that's a risk worth taking.'

CHAPTER EIGHT

A RISK worth taking? Emily couldn't believe she'd said that. If Jude kissed her now—

Too late. Jude was already kissing her—and from the moment his lips touched hers, her fears no longer made any kind of sense. He kissed her slow and easy, calming her and soothing her scampering heartbeat.

She'd become so scared during the strip, starting out gamely and confidently, then beginning to think she'd made the hugest blunder of her life.

Now, with his strong arms holding her, warm and secure, Jude's lips worked a special magic, sending golden heat through her, down her arms, pooling low in her stomach.

Relaxed and dreamy, she gave up worrying about risks and simply sank into this bliss—savouring the strength of his arms about her, revelling in the manly texture of his jaw against hers.

He'd turned the tables on her this evening. She'd started out trying to surprise him, but now he was the one taking control. With a hand buried in her hair, he held her just where he wanted her and took the kiss deeper.

Oh, man. Her knees almost gave way. They were like two notes blending in perfect harmony, building to a joint crescendo.

Her dress fell apart and his touch on her breasts through their thin covering of lace was so sexy their kiss turned molten.

She thought fleetingly of Michael and a flash of panic flared. Then she leant back and looked into Jude's sexy grey eyes, and she saw gravity and tenderness mixed with his desire.

Her panic subsided. This was OK. It really was OK. Their passion was fuelled by so much more than simple lust. Yes, her heart was involved, but she was quite clear-headed. This night was all about hope and courage, and the soul-deep need for two human beings to connect.

Against her ear, Jude murmured, 'You know I can't make promises about the future.'

'Shh.' She pressed a finger to his lips. 'I understand, Jude, and I'm not asking for promises.'

She couldn't deny she was in love with him. Painfully, wonderfully in love. But Jude had put his life on hold, and she would, too. For the first time, she was offering her love without an accompanying dream of ever after. It was such a relief to simply be with him without the weight of expectation.

Winding her arms around his neck, she kissed the underside of his jaw. 'I vote we make this a night to remember.'

It was all the invitation Jude needed. Scooping her effortlessly into his arms, he carried her down the hallway to the big double bed.

At last.

They'd been dancing around this for days, trying to resist, but now it felt so good to let the barriers fall. So right to let the world retreat, to allow their emotions to swell and their longing to build, till just the two of them existed.

Now. Here. This.

Sweet journey of discovery.

As they lay close together in the darkness, Jude was tormented by questions.

Why did I find her now?

Why her?
Why now?

He'd been falling hard and fast for Emily from the moment he set eyes on her. Within no time he'd become addicted, needing to watch her at work in the kitchen, to chat with her about his books, to chat with her about anything, really, share his favourite view…

And now, after loving him with a passion and honesty that utterly enslaved him, she was lying beside him in the darkness, with her round little rump settled against his hip, her foot hooked possessively over his calf, her breathing soft and even…

And he wanted more. Wanted to make her his own, to keep her by his side.

Emily had asked him once if he would give up his lifestyle for the right woman. Now, he was beginning to suspect she was that woman, and he was quite sure he would do anything. He wanted to offer her the world…

But all he had to offer was a gaping black hole filled with question marks.

With a heavy sigh, he tried to fight off his thoughts of what lay ahead of him. To counter them, he replayed precious images in his mind. The fall of lamplight on Emily's soft white curves. The fiery shimmer of her hair on the pillow. The adorable perfection of her pale pink-tipped breasts.

The other gifts she offered for his senses, the wild-flower scent of her skin, her silky softness, the intoxicating sweetness of her kisses, her heartbeats knocking against his.

He wanted it all.

Morning sunlight filtered softly through the curtains.

Emily lay on her side, not wanting to disturb Jude, not wanting to think how rash she'd been to sleep with this man.

She had no regrets. Last night had been beyond wonderful, and today was all about Jude. She mustn't spoil it by worrying about where this would take her.

For now, she was very happy to feast her eyes on him, and there was much to admire. Even when he was asleep, his face was strong, with a largish nose, not too pointy or too fleshy, dark eyebrows and a long jaw, now covered in morning stubble.

The duvet had slipped and she let her gaze drift over his bare torso—over his wide muscled shoulders and solid chest, his flat stomach, no doubt toned from all that hiking he did.

She thought about the day ahead of him, and a wave of fear eddied through her. She couldn't bear to think of Jude's precious, clever brain being interfered with by surgeons' scalpels. Quickly, she pushed those thoughts aside and dwelled instead on the amazing night they'd shared.

Amidst the emotion and dizzying passion, there'd been sweet moments of intimate connection, so beautiful and tender that she'd almost wept. Thank heavens she'd held back on the tears, for Jude's sake. She wanted only happy memories for him.

Now, also for Jude's sake, her task was to stay upbeat today, *all day*, even though she was as scared as she'd ever been.

It helped to remember her grandmother's words. *You just need to put yourself in Jude's shoes. Follow your instincts and I'm sure you'll work out the best way to keep his spirits up.*

Emily smiled at this. She wondered what Granny Silver would think if she knew her advice had led her granddaughter to attempt a striptease. Truth was, there'd been a double benefit. Not just for Jude but for her as well. For the first time she'd taken an impulsive risk, and wow, hadn't it been worth it?

In the past, she'd always been a bit inhibited in her relationships. She'd been aware of *something* holding her back and, deep down, she'd known that she'd disappointed her boyfriends— even Michael.

Given this history, it was quite amazing that she'd attempted something as bold as a striptease for Jude. Perhaps the secret was that she'd been totally focused on his needs. Her own disappointments with boyfriends had made her ultra-careful, but last night she'd thought only of Jude, and she'd been determined to give him something fun to remember.

Now that she thought about it, she supposed the striptease was the kind of challenge Jude's heroines might have taken on.

How about that?

And look at the result—the most wonderful night of her life. She might even be able to think of herself as a winner at last.

Slipping out of bed, she pulled on her night-gown, the old-fashioned cream and lace frills one that Jude had said made her look like an angel, and she padded out to the kitchen to make breakfast.

He was awake when she returned with a tray, and he greeted her with a happy grin. 'Ah, my favourite nightgown. This morning with that tray, you make me think of Florence Nightingale.'

'I don't have a lamp.'

'No, you have a coffee pot, which is even better.'

Indeed it was. They sat in bed propped against a bank of pillows, sipping big mugs of coffee and munching on blueberry pancakes topped with lightly fried sliced bananas.

Emily had drawn the curtains wide to give them a clear view of the morning sky and the Brisbane River wandering slowly between forests of skyscrapers. They felt rather smug as they listened to the sounds of the city traffic and the poor workers hurrying to their offices, which was ironic considering what lay ahead for Jude. But he seemed quite relaxed.

Emily wondered if he was faking this calmness. For her own part, she was finding it increasingly hard to keep up a brave face. Every time she looked at the clock and saw the time creeping closer to the fateful hour of three o'clock, the time Jude was to be admitted, she felt a fresh download of dread.

After breakfast, Jude wandered down to the shops to buy a newspaper or two, and Emily tried to keep busy, washing the breakfast things by hand, even though there was a dishwasher. She also dried the dishes and put them away, and wiped down the benches and polished them until they shone. Still feeling restless, she swept the floor.

Several times, she wanted to ask Jude if there was anything she could do for him, but she knew he'd packed everything he needed for the hospital, including his laptop.

'You never know, I might get some writing done. Better to be optimistic than the alternative.' He'd said this with a cheeky wink that made her throat ache.

For lunch Emily made toasted cheese sandwiches and heated one of Jude's collection of tinned soups—rich tomato and basil. Afterwards, she was standing at the sink, once again rinsing plates, when Jude came up behind her.

Looping his arms about her, he hugged her, holding her against his chest—and Emily loved it.

She could remember when she was a child, watching her dad come up and hug her mum this way. Her mum would be tired, with no make-up or fancy clothes, but he'd kiss her neck and ask fondly, 'How's my favourite girl?'

Her mum, who'd also worked as hard on their farm as her dad, used to pretend to be too busy and brush him off. But she'd give him a quick kiss, and she'd smile to herself and hum happily under her breath as she peeled potatoes or sliced beans.

Emily had grown up wanting a husband like that, someone who liked to hug her at any old time of the day.

Now, as Jude pressed his lips to the nape of

her neck, she closed her eyes, relishing the reassuring warmth of his arms about her and the
familiar intimacy of the gesture.

'I want you to do me a favour this afternoon,'
he said, still with his arms around her waist.

Emily nodded, eager to please. 'Of course.
How can I help?'

'I want you to go to your grandmother's and
stay there for the next few days.'

No!

She went cold all over, and only remembered
just in time to bite back a wailing protest. She
didn't want to do or say anything to upset Jude
today, but crikey, he was upsetting her. She
thought he'd given up on this desire to keep her
away, but he was asking her to step out of his
life at this most crucial time. It was hard not to
panic.

She drew a deep breath, praying for calm. 'I
can't just drop you off at the hospital and walk
away as if I don't care.'

Jude's arms tensed, and then they dropped to
his sides as he stepped away. Fighting panic,
Emily turned to face him and her heart trembled

when she saw the resolve in his eyes and the determined set of his mouth. He was serious.

'I don't want you hanging around the hospital, Emily. I couldn't bear to think of you sitting around in some dreary waiting room tomorrow, while I'm in the theatre. I'll give the staff your name as a contact, and you can ring when it's all over to see how I'm doing.'

'But I don't mind waiting.' A pleading note crept into her voice. But she sensed that wouldn't work with Jude, so she forced a smile and tried another tack. 'Honestly, I have a couple of fabulous books to read. I've found this fantastic thriller writer, you see, and he keeps me glued to the page and—'

'Emily, listen.' Stepping forward again, Jude grasped her shoulders and his eyes were storm-grey serious. Then his expression softened and he said gently, 'I'll feel so much better if I know you're away from there.'

'But I won't feel better.'

'You will,' he insisted in that same quiet voice. 'Do this for me.' The ghost of a smile crept into his eyes. 'I want to picture you sitting on a beach, watching the waves roll in, or going for walks beside the water with your hair blowing in the wind.'

His big hands squeezed her shoulders. 'Granny Silver will be much better company tomorrow than a hospital waiting room. And tonight I want to think of you going to sleep listening to the sea.'

But couldn't he understand that, for her, leaving him alone felt like the worst kind of desertion? Yet another rejection?

Admittedly, she hadn't been looking forward to waiting at the hospital—she hated it at the best of times—but she'd been determined to be there for Jude.

But perhaps she should have expected this reaction from Jude. He was behaving the way his father had, not wanting others to see him weakened or helpless.

He hadn't told any of his friends about his health problems until Alex had sent them prompting text messages. And it made sense that a man as independent as Jude was would hate the idea of a woman hanging about the hospital ward, feeling sorry for him.

He was probably also worried that she'd con-

sider them a couple after last night, but he'd offered no promises and she'd pledged to respect
his wishes.

Blinking to banish the threat of tears, she managed to smile. 'OK, I'll stay away from the hospital, on one condition.'

'Not another condition?' A silvery light glis-
tened in Jude's grey eyes. 'What is it?'

Stepping closer, she linked her arms around
his neck. 'One last kiss. For luck.'

'Emily.'

Her name was a whispered prayer as he drew
her into his arms and his warm, pliant lips met
hers in a perfect kiss—tender and beautiful and
utterly close-your-eyes-and-go-to-heaven blissful.

She could feel his heart thundering against her
and she wished, more than anything, that they
could simply skip over these next twenty-four
hours. She was gripped by a terrible feeling of
powerlessness and she pressed her cheek against
Jude's chest and hugged him close.

There were so many things she wanted to tell
him—that he was a truly wonderful man, that
he was going to come through this just fine, that

no matter what happened, she would be there waiting for him.

But she kept these thoughts to herself. She wasn't sure he wanted to hear promises that sounded suspiciously like love.

They left early for the hospital, driving in Jude's car, which he insisted Emily use when she continued on to her grandmother's.

Their route took them past the park, and Emily wondered aloud if the heron was there again today.

Jude grinned. 'We have time. Why don't we take a look?'

They were in luck, finding a parking spot close to the gates, so it was no time before they were following the path that wound through a grove of jacarandas.

But as they rounded the bend, the pond was disappointingly empty of herons.

There were ducks on the water and a few children throwing food to them, but no long-legged white bird wading in the shallows.

'Maybe he's turned back into an alien?' Emily said to lighten the moment. She knew it was silly to feel disappointed. There was nothing symbolic about the heron. It wasn't as if he was a good omen or anything, but now she wished she hadn't suggested looking for him.

She was turning away when Jude said, 'Look.'

He was smiling as he pointed—and, sure enough, emerging from a clump of reeds, appearing quite dazzling in the sunlight, came the heron.

'He's like you,' Emily said.

Jude looked at her in surprise. 'Really? How?'

'He's bit of a loner.'

He laughed and a smile lingered as they walked back to the car. For some reason she couldn't quite explain, Emily felt just a little braver.

She was very proud that she didn't cry when she said goodbye at the hospital entrance. It was all over in a moment. Jude hugged her so tightly she could hardly breathe, then he grabbed his leather overnight bag and flashed a quick smile.

'See you in a while.'

With a final cheeky wink that just about broke her heart, he turned and strode through the swinging glass doors.

* * *

On the expressway to the Sunshine Coast there were very few places for Emily to pull over, so she couldn't allow herself to cry. She wouldn't help Jude by blinding herself with tears and having an accident, so she listened to music on the radio and tried not to think about him.

Having rung her grandmother earlier, she was expected, and at the first available shopping centre she bought a bunch of flowers and ingredients for a few meals.

She would enjoy cooking, and it would give Granny Silver a break. She bought chocolates, too, and a bottle of Granny's favourite sherry, and then she drove on, looking forward to the moment she crested the final rise and saw her first glimpse of the sea.

This last leg of the journey had always excited her. But today when she saw the curling blue waves, she could only think about Jude and her spirits refused to lift. Even the sight of her grandmother's cottage hunkering beneath a big old cassia tree brought only the tiniest sense of relief.

As soon as she parked in the driveway, the cottage door opened and Granny Silver was there waiting, arms ready to hug her. Emily's eyes filled with tears, but she still had to stay strong. She couldn't dissolve into tears on the footpath in full view of her grandmother's neighbours.

Taking a deep breath, she climbed out, hauled her bags and her shopping from the back seat and closed the car doors with her hip before walking with her arms full up the crazy-paving path.

'You're weighed down, there,' Granny said. 'Can I help with anything?'

Emily shook her head. 'I've got it all balanced, thanks. I'll take the shopping straight through to the kitchen. OK?'

'Of course, dear.'

Stepping through the doorway into the dearly loved front room, Emily saw its deep chintz-covered armchairs and lush pot plants and dozens of family photographs. She caught the faint smell of dried lavender and the lump in her throat swelled to the size of a grapefruit.

Here she was, surrounded by so much that she loved, while Jude was alone in Brisbane in a hospital ward...waiting...

She managed to dump the groceries on the kitchen counter before her tears fell.

In torrents.

'I'm so sorry,' she spluttered to her concerned grandmother, but she couldn't explain. All she could do was collapse into an armchair and weep… For Jude, for herself…and for the unknown future…

CHAPTER NINE

'SO IT seems that your friendship with Jude is rather special after all,' Granny Silver said gently.

'It is and it isn't.' Emily released a slow sigh, not sure how she could explain now that she'd apologised for her tears and washed her face, and was leaning back against her grandmother's embroidered cushions.

They were drinking a post-tears cup of tea and she knew an explanation was expected.

'Jude's a really wonderful guy, so of course I really like him, Granny. But this is a very scary thing that's happening to him, and he's determined to deal with it on his own.'

'That's hard on you.'

'Yes. I hoped I'd be stronger.'

'Try not to worry too much, Emily. A friend of mine had a similar operation at the same hospital and apparently the neurosurgeons there are all wonderful. I don't think you should be too concerned.'

'That's good to know. Jude doesn't say much, but I know he's freaked about the possibility of blindness.' Emily looked at her grandmother with a shaky smile. 'But if the surgeon's excellent, Jude should be fine, shouldn't he?'

'Exactly, my dear.'

The next morning, the day of Jude's operation, Emily was far too restless and tense to hang about the house. She needed to take a really long walk, and she needed to be alone.

'Of course, I understand,' Granny Silver assured her. 'Off you go. I'll say a prayer for Jude.'

It was a beautiful day with a brilliant, cloudless blue sky and rolling, sunlit surf. Emily walked along the sand to the far end of Sunshine Beach and then climbed the track over the headland into Noosa National Park. It felt somehow appropriate to be climbing on this particular day. The ascent was fairly sedate and she stayed on the beaten track, but she felt as if she were climbing for Jude.

From the top of the headland she caught sight

of porpoises leaping and frolicking in clear green waves, and they looked so lively and cheerful she couldn't help smiling.

She continued on to Hell's Gates, a steep narrow canyon of rocks where the sea rushed in, wild and rough and foaming. Usually she was fascinated by the crashing waves and the shooting spray. Today the sense of danger made her skin crawl and she turned away, choosing a sandy track that wound away from the sea through friendly bushland.

Always, with every step, she thought of Jude.

It was so awful to think of him lying on an operating table, beneath bright lights and surrounded by people in masks, holding scalpels. Each time an image from the operating theatre flashed through her mind, she was sluiced by hot fear.

Hastily, she substituted happier memories. Jude striding purposefully up the track to Sunset Ridge. Jude laughing with her as they invented crazy theories about the white heron. The silvery warmth in his eyes just before he kissed her.

It was impossible to pretend that she wasn't in love with him. She'd tried walking around that fact and dressing it up in other names, telling herself that as far as Jude was concerned, she was a stand-in for Alex, or a caring friend, or simply…a female distraction.

Once again, she'd actively tried to resist falling in love. It was way too soon. She'd just run away from a disastrous relationship and she knew all too well that, for her, romance was a shortcut to misery. The very words *in love* brought every one of her trust issues bursting to the surface.

Not that she had a good reason to mistrust Jude. He'd gone out of his way to make his position crystal clear. He wasn't available for a new relationship, and even if he had been available, he'd intimated that he had a history of avoiding long-term commitment.

In her head, Emily was totally OK with this. She certainly wasn't looking at Jude as future husband material. She'd archived that dream where it belonged—with the Tooth Fairy and Santa Claus. *And* she'd tried her best to keep her heart strong and safe but, whether she liked it or not, she'd become emotionally involved with Jude. On all kinds of levels.

Small wonder he'd sent her away yesterday.

He probably hoped that distance would bring her to her senses.

Just as she reached this miserable conclusion, the track emerged out of bushland into a burst of sunshine and a view of a gorgeous cove. Emily found a flat rock to sit on and looked down at the rocky cliffs, the pale yellow sand and the clear, clear water in three shades of aquamarine.

She'd worn a long-sleeved shirt to protect her from the sun, and now she peeled the cuff back to check her watch.

It was eleven-thirty, and Jude's operation should be almost over.

Sickening fear churned in her stomach. *Please, let him be OK.*

Worries crowded in, and she found herself imagining what his life would be like if his optic nerve was damaged and he lost his sight. So many things he wouldn't see—sunsets, wading herons, mountain views, words on a page...or on a computer screen...

Closing her eyes, she hugged her knees. 'Hang in there, Jude. You're going to be fine. You'll be better than ever when this is over.'

Taking a deep breath, she opened her eyes and

saw a white-breasted eagle swooping down from the heights, curving in a majestic pure loop, right in front of her.

Jude loved birds and, although Emily wasn't normally superstitious, she couldn't help hoping that this eagle was a sign that all was well.

Bending down, she picked a wild flower from a clump growing at the base of the rock she was sitting on. The flower was a small daisy, nondescript and pale brown, but she threaded it through the band of her sunhat and set off again, her heart once more hopeful.

'Good afternoon. I'm ringing to enquire about Jude Marlowe. He had surgery this morning.'

'Jude Marlowe,' a young woman's voice repeated. 'And your name is?'

'Emily Silver. I believe Jude left my name as a contact.'

'We have Charlotte Kenney listed here as Mr Marlowe's next of kin.'

'Yes, that's Jude's sister.' Despite her nerves, Emily tried to speak calmly. 'But I understand he was also going to leave my name.'

'Let me see… Can you hold the line, please? I'll be back in one moment.'

Emily felt sick as she waited, clutching the phone, while a thousand scenarios flashed through her head. She wondered if Jude had forgotten to leave her name. Or, worse, that he'd changed his mind and no longer wanted her to be informed about him. Or the very worst possibility—something awful had happened and the nurse needed permission to tell Emily about it.

'Hello, this is Dr Keira Arnold.'

A doctor? Fear exploded in Emily's face. *Was this bad news? Please, no.*

'I believe you'd like an update on Jude Marlowe's condition,' the doctor said.

'Yes.' Emily's throat was so tight she could barely squeeze the word out. 'Please.'

'So you're Emily Silver?'

'That's right.'

'It's good to speak to you, Emily. I'm an old friend of Jude's.'

'A friend?' Emily gulped. Her first thought was that Jude must be OK. Surely this doctor wouldn't be chatting about friendships if there was a problem. Then another thought clicked.

Was she speaking to the owner of the hiking boots? 'Are you Keira, the Army doctor?'

'Yes, that's right. I'm actually Major Arnold, but pulling rank doesn't go down too well in a civilian hospital.'

So this was the attractive dark-haired woman in Jude's alpine photo, the former girlfriend who regularly returned to his home.

Keira Arnold said, 'Fortunately, my leave has coincided with Jude's op, so I've been able to keep a friendly eye on him from the wings, so to speak.'

Emily's head was buzzing with a gazillion questions, but there was only one that really mattered. 'How is he?'

'The operation went very well. The neurosurgeon is exceptionally experienced, for which I'm grateful. Jude came out of the recovery room a short while ago and he's in good spirits.'

Emily let out a shuddering whoosh of relief. 'That's wonderful. What about his vision? Is that OK?'

'I'm afraid it's too early to tell.'

'Oh…I see.'

There were so many questions Emily wanted to

ask, but she'd sensed a subtle vibe coming from this other woman. Despite the surface friendliness, there was an atmosphere that smacked of power play. Emily had experienced plenty of this in the course of her work at the bank but, under these circumstances, she wasn't quite sure what to make of it.

Opting for caution, she said simply, 'Thanks for telling me. I'm very relieved and if you're speaking to Jude, please tell him I called and give him my…my love.'

'Of course.'

'And I'd appreciate hearing—if there's any more news.'

'All right. We'll keep in touch. Oh, and by the way—' the doctor's voice dropped to a confidential purr '—congratulations on your engagement. I'm pleased that Jude's finally taking the plunge.'

She promptly hung up.

And Emily almost dropped her phone.

Engagement? What engagement?

How on earth had the doctor arrived at that crazy conclusion? Jude would never have suggested such a thing.

It was downright *weird.* And unsettling.

Emily was shaking her head as she went through to the kitchen where her grandmother was adding fresh water to a vase of flowers.

Granny turned, her eyes cautious, yet eager for news.

'Jude seems to be fine,' Emily said.

'Oh, darling, what a relief.' It wasn't long, however, before her grandmother was frowning. 'You don't look happy. Is there something else?'

'I'm very happy. Truly, I'm thrilled.' Emily gave a dazed shake of her head. 'But, for some reason I don't understand, the people at the hospital think I'm Jude's fiancée.'

'How interesting.'

'It's rubbish, of course. We've only known each other for about two weeks.'

'A lot can happen in two weeks.' Granny straightened an iris, then stood back to admire the arrangement Emily had bought for her yesterday.

'Jude and I haven't had a whirlwind romance, if that's what you're thinking.' Emily stooped to pick up a fallen petal from the floor. The action helped to hide her guilty flush from her granny's searching gaze. 'It's possible that the hospital wouldn't pass on any news unless I was a wife or a fiancée, so perhaps Jude fudged the truth.'

'Yes, that might be the story. Or perhaps it's wishful thinking on his part?'

'Granny—' Emily sent her a withering look '—when did you become such a hopeless romantic?'

'A few decades before you did, my dear. I'm afraid I may have passed on the gene.'

They shared a rueful smile.

'Actually, that's a sore point,' Emily admitted. Pulling out a kitchen stool, she plumped down on it, resting her elbows on the bench. 'I fall in love far too easily, and then I leave myself wide open to be hurt.'

'Are you saying that you don't trust your own feelings?'

'Maybe. I certainly don't understand how love happens so easily for everyone else and I find it so hard. Even when I'm convinced I've found someone perfect, he can turn out to be a dud.'

Lifting her gloomy gaze, Emily saw her grandmother's shocked face. 'I don't mean Jude. There was…someone else.'

Granny accepted this with a thoughtful nod. Then she asked carefully, 'How would you feel about Jude if he did lose his sight?'

The most awful ache bloomed in Emily's heart. 'I'd be devastated for him,' she said softly. 'But it wouldn't change how I feel about him.'

No matter what happened to Jude, she would feel this same deep emotional bond with him. And if this sense of connection and caring wasn't love, Emily didn't know what it was.

'But Jude's a loner, Granny. Even if he was perfectly well, he wouldn't be looking for a long-term relationship.'

'A loner?' Granny Silver's eyes widened. 'That surprises me. He has such a warm and engaging personality. Are you sure he's a true loner?'

'He has a definite reclusive streak, although I must admit he was a very hospitable host, in spite of everything else going on in his life.'

'Perhaps he's just waiting for the right woman, dear.'

Emily rolled her eyes to the ceiling. 'That's what he says.'

But I'm not holding out hope that I could be her.

Despite that last wonderful night together, Jude

had sent her away, as if he was already preparing her for an eventual permanent separation.

Once again she'd fallen too quickly and too easily for a man who was, ultimately, no more suitable for her than Michael had been—or Dave, or Dimitri, for that matter.

Climbing from the stool, she went to the pantry. 'I think I'll make a bacon-and-macaroni casserole.'

Granny's eyes met hers and they shared another smile. They both knew very well that since Emily's early childhood, whenever she was anxious or disappointed or hurt, this dish was her number one comfort food.

It was the middle of the next morning when Jude rang. Emily saw his name on her screen and her heart leapt like a kite in a wind gust.

'Hi, Jude.' Her voice was all fluttery. 'How are you?'

'Not too bad, thanks.'

It was so-o-o good to hear his voice and to know he really was OK. She held the phone close to her ear, as if it could somehow strengthen the contact. 'So everything's going well?'

'Apparently I'm on track. The physio's just taken me for a walk, and I wasn't too doddery.'

'Fantastic. How are your eyes?'

There was a beat before he answered. 'Hard to say. I've been told to be patient. How are you?'

'I...I'm absolutely fine.' *Missing you.*

'*Where* are you?'

'On the beach, actually.'

'Sunbathing in a bikini?'

He asked this in such a hopeful, boyish tone that Emily laughed.

'No, Jude. I'm a redhead, remember? I don't sunbathe. I'm lying on the sand, reading one of your books, but I'm in the shade and I'm wearing a boring sunhat and a long-sleeved top.'

'Very wise of you,' he said warmly. 'It'd be a crime to burn your lovely complexion.'

Encouraged by this, Emily said, 'I rang the hospital yesterday and I spoke to Dr Keira Arnold.'

'Yes, Keira mentioned you'd called. I hope she set your mind at rest.'

'She told me your surgeon was top-notch and that everything went well, so of course I was incredibly relieved. But one thing was odd, Jude. Keira thinks we're engaged.'

'Ah...yes. Sorry about that.' There was a small throat-clearing noise. 'I told a white lie to the front desk. They're nervous about giving patient information to anyone outside the family. But don't worry; I've now set Keira straight.'

'Right.' Emily ignored the sinking feeling in her stomach. 'Glad to hear it.' She wondered if Keira Arnold had already known this and had been playing with her.

'So when can I come to visit you?' Emily asked.

There was an unsettling silence.

'Can you hold off for a day or so?' Jude said at last.

'It...it's up to you, of course.' She hoped he couldn't hear her disappointment. 'I'll call you tomorrow, OK?'

'Yes, do that. I'll look forward to it.'

After she disconnected, Emily sat staring out at the sea, watching wave after wave roll in and crash in a fringe of frothing foam. She told herself she should be glad Jude was well. That was all that mattered.

But even though his recovery was the only thing that really mattered, it couldn't quite heal her niggling unease over Keira Arnold. The woman had a carte blanche invitation to stay at Jude's home any time she fancied *and* she was, apparently, at his bedside night and day, holding his hand, mopping his brow, doing the whole Florence Nightingale act while Emily had been sent into exile.

Exactly what kind of ex-girlfriend was this Keira? Was she still angling to become Jude's *Mrs Right*?

Hospitals, Jude decided, were the least private places in the world. There was always someone coming through his doorway—a tea lady, an orderly, a nurse, a doctor...

He barely got five minutes to string his thoughts together. Although that was possibly a good thing. Left alone, he'd spend far too much time thinking about Emily.

Even with the interruptions, he still found himself replaying snatches of their many conversations in his head, remembering the delightful sparkle in her eyes when she talked.

The more intimate memories damn near broke his heart.

Every moment he'd spent with Emily—in the apartment, or downtown, or in the mountains—seemed to be lit up in neon lights. His life was divided into two parts: before and after meeting Emily.

And now *this*…

This frustrating, humiliating illness.

It was all very well for the doctors to assure him that he'd be fine. In time. Right now, his head was a field of pain and his sight was scarily blurred. He had to wait six weeks for an MRI to determine the true success of the op.

Was it too long to expect Emily to wait?

The next day, gently encouraged by Granny Silver, Emily rang Jude and adopted the assertive tones she used in her office on a daily basis.

'I'm bringing Granny to Brisbane to collect her new glasses, so I'll call in and see you while I'm nearby.' Without giving Jude a chance to object, she went on, 'It would be silly to come all that way and not say hello.'

Jude agreed, but with less enthusiasm than she

would have liked, and she arrived early in the afternoon, heart thumping unnecessarily hard as she reached the door to his private room.

A grey-haired man and woman were just leaving.

Somehow, Emily hadn't expected this. Slightly bewildered, she nodded to them and they smiled and nodded back.

As she rounded the doorway, she saw Jude sitting in a chair in the corner, dressed not in pyjamas but in jeans and a white shirt, open at the neck, sleeves rolled up, looking very much his usual hunky self, except that he was wearing dark glasses.

There was a young woman in a chair next to him. Her hair was a mass of dark shiny curls and she was leaning close, holding Jude's hand.

Emily told herself she didn't care if this was another of Jude's ex-girlfriends. Just the same, her knees began to shake.

Then the other woman saw her. She dropped Jude's hand and smiled. 'Here's another visitor. You're popular today, Jude.'

He tensed, turning his head to the door.

Emily had no idea if he could see her. 'Hello, Jude.' Her voice was as shaky as her knees.

'Emily.' He stood quickly, but he wasn't smiling.

'I'm Charlotte,' the woman next to him said, stepping forward and smiling as she held out her hand. 'Jude's sister.'

His sister? Of course. Why hadn't she thought of that? Pumped with relief, Emily grinned at them both. 'Nice to meet you, Charlotte.'

'I'm so glad to meet you,' Charlotte responded. 'Jude's been telling me how much he's enjoyed your company.'

'Has he?' Emily almost floated into the room and her grin was probably ridiculously wide as she shook Charlotte's hand. Then she kissed Jude's cheek, catching a quick heady whiff of his delicious aftershave.

'You look really well,' she told him. 'You look fantastic.'

'Thanks.' His mouth tilted, not quite making a smile.

Clearly, he wasn't as thrilled to see her as his sister was.

'I wasn't sure what to bring,' Emily said, trying not to sound too easily deflated by Jude's grimness. 'I settled for grapes and dark chocolate.' She turned to put them on the bedside table. 'Oh, I see you already have grapes *and* chocolate.'

'Sid Johnson brought them,' Charlotte said. 'The old police friend of Jude's who's just left.' And then she smiled, defusing the awkward moment. 'Great minds think alike.'

'Can't have too much of grapes and chocolate,' Jude added gallantly. And then, politely, 'Emily, take a seat.'

'No, I'm fine, thanks.' Jude was the patient—she couldn't take his seat.

'I'll hop back on the bed.' Already Jude was walking over to the bed, but his movements were super-careful and, when he sat, he grimaced slightly as he swung his legs up and settled against the pillows.

It was unsettling to see him moving so cautiously when just a few days ago he'd climbed a mountain with effortless ease. Emily realised she'd been holding her breath as she watched him. Her gaze met Charlotte's and she could see that his sister shared her disquiet.

Charlotte was warm and friendly, however, drawing Emily into the conversation, and the three of them were soon chatting quite congenially.

Charlotte filled Jude in on her family's news. Her eldest, Sophie, had started ballet lessons. Oliver skinned his knee falling off his trike. Daisy would soon be walking.

Jude was much more relaxed and smiling as he listened to her, and his questions about his nieces and nephew revealed genuine interest rather than mere politeness.

Emily told him about her walk through the Noosa National Park, how she'd seen porpoises and an eagle.

'A white-breasted sea eagle?'

'Probably. I'm not great on identification, but it was certainly white and it was beautiful. I decided it was a good omen.'

'I'm sure it was,' said Charlotte warmly, but Jude made no comment.

'I've also had a brilliant idea for an online business,' Emily said, too excited to keep this news to herself.

Jude turned to her, clearly interested. 'Come on, tell us.'

'The idea hit me yesterday while I was watching mothers and children playing on the beach—'

'Well, what's this?' interrupted a voice from the doorway. 'The Jude Marlowe fan club?'

Emily turned as yet another young woman entered the room. Tall as a model, and wearing a neat navy trouser suit, she wore her dark hair pulled back from her intelligently attractive face. Emily instantly recognised her as the woman in the photo at Jude's place—Dr Keira Arnold.

Keira didn't wait for Jude's introduction. 'I'm guessing you must be Emily,' she said, breezing into the room. 'I'm Keira. We met over the phone.'

As she shook Emily's hand she let her keen dark gaze linger for a shade too long, as if she were sizing her up. Then she turned to Jude, smiling.

'Move over,' she ordered him and she sat on his bed, nudging his legs with her bottom, very much at ease.

Emily hung on to her smile—*just*—and she thought she heard a small huff that might have been reproach from Jude's sister. Shooting a quick glance Charlotte's way, she caught her fleeting raised-eyebrow look of sympathy.

Apparently she had an ally, which was interesting. Grateful for small mercies, Emily took a deep breath and secured her smile more firmly. But there was an awkward atmosphere in the room now that hadn't been there before.

'Emily was telling us about a new business idea,' Charlotte told Keira.

'Oh? Do tell…'

'It's OK,' Emily said uneasily. 'I can fill Jude in with the details some other time.'

Similarly, Charlotte's chatter about her family seemed to have dried up and Jude, for his part, looked tired.

Their conversation was reduced to unexciting small talk about the traffic on the freeway, the length of Charlotte's stay in Brisbane and the weather. After less than five minutes, Charlotte looked at her watch, then jumped to her feet.

'If you'll excuse me, I really must hurry to make a phone call. I've just remembered something I need to remind my babysitter about.' She kissed Jude and gave him a gentle hug. 'See you later, big brother.'

She sent Emily a warm smile. 'Lovely to meet you.' Impulsively, she gave Emily a hug, too. 'I might not see you again before I leave tomorrow, so let me thank you now for taking such great care of Jude.'

Surprised, Emily wondered what Jude had told his sister. Judging by Keira's dark expression, she may have been pondering the same question.

After Charlotte left, the conversation might have become really awkward if Jude hadn't yawned.

Emily took this as her cue. 'You need to rest, Jude, and I should be on my way. Granny Silver is probably ready and waiting for me.'

Jude smiled. 'How is Granny?'

'As sprightly as ever. She sends her best wishes.'

This time, when she kissed Jude's cheek, she was uncomfortably aware of Keira watching them.

'Take care,' she told him softly.

'You, too,' Jude murmured.

Before she could draw away, his hand closed

around her wrist, holding her close to him. His lips brushed her cheek again in a deliberate unhurried caress. 'Thanks for coming,' he murmured. 'You're a breath of fresh air.'

It was ridiculous that such brief, sweet contact with him could set Emily's skin flaming. Unfortunately, the knowledge that she was being watched by his ex made the flames even hotter.

Gamely, she flashed Keira a brilliant smile. 'Bye, and nice to meet you.'

Outside in the hallway, she let out her breath in a whoosh of relief. Visiting Jude had been so much harder than she'd expected.

His remoteness had been disconcerting, but she'd also been puzzled by his relationship with Keira Arnold. What was this woman's role, exactly? Control freak, or extremely close and caring friend?

Or was she still in love with Jude?

'Emily?'

Keira's voice sounded behind her. *Talk of the devil.* Emily took a quick breath before she turned.

'Can I have a word?' the doctor asked.

Emily gulped. What was this about? She smiled. 'Yes, of course.'

'We can talk in here.' Keira pushed open a door, revealing a small, surprisingly empty sitting room with vinyl seats, a rack of tattered magazines and a coffee machine in the corner.

Emily's stomach tightened. Why the seclusion? Was Keira going to grill her about her connection to Jude? Would she quiz her about the fake engagement?

'Would you like a coffee?' Keira asked.

Emily shook her head. 'I don't have long. My grandmother's waiting.'

'Of course.' Keira sat, crossing her long athletic legs, and she indicated for Emily to take a chair opposite. 'This won't take a moment, but I wanted to talk to you about Jude's recovery.'

Instantly alarmed, Emily sat forward. 'Is there a problem? He'll be OK, won't he?'

'Physically, he's on track to make a fine recovery,' Keira began with a watchful smile. 'It would help, though, if he didn't feel compelled to play the tough guy. In the Army, I deal with men like Jude all the time. They keep their problems, particularly their medical problems, to themselves. It's part of the masculine thing. To bottle it up.'

Emily nodded, and wondered again where this was leading.

'Believe me,' Keira continued, 'I've seen a lot of hardened men serving in dangerous situations and it's the guys who play it cool who often suffer the greatest emotional pain when they're suddenly helpless. They *hate* to lose control.'

'I know Jude's very worried about his eyesight.'

'Of course he is. The risk of going blind is a huge deal for him. It would be for anyone.'

'Is there still a risk?' Emily pressed her hands over the sudden painful ache in her chest.

'To be honest, I don't think there's a huge risk now. His vision's still very blurry, but that should settle down, if he takes it easy. I see my role as trying to keep him calm, which is important.'

With a self-satisfied smile, Keira said, 'I'm just so glad I took leave this week. I usually stay at Jude's mountain retreat, clearing my head in the fresh air and the rainforest, but I'm so pleased I can keep a professional eye on him now. I don't have to be back with my unit for another ten days.'

Ten days?

Just in time, Emily stifled a gasp of dismay. 'I thought he'd be out of hospital in a day or two.'

'He will, but he'll need ongoing professional care.'

Emily had planned to do any necessary caring. She could stay on at Alex's apartment for at least another week, and she'd imagined cooking for Jude and possibly reading the paper to him until his vision cleared. She could take him to the park and they'd go for walks together. Each day they'd walk a little further and he'd grow stronger.

'My plan,' said Keira, 'is to get him out of hospital as soon as possible. I've already spoken to his surgeon and he agrees that Jude will do much better in familiar surroundings. The mountain is a bit isolated in terms of any post-op problems, though, so I think your cousin's place is the best option. I'll stay on until things have fully stabilised.'

But there are only two bedrooms in Alex's apartment.

'I'm used to kipping down on stretchers,' Keira added, as if she'd already guessed the direction of Emily's thoughts. 'I'll monitor the severity of Jude's headaches and make sure that he either wears his dark glasses or stays in a semi-darkened room.'

These tasks didn't sound particularly difficult to Emily, certainly not matters that required the skills of a fully qualified Army surgeon. But if she questioned Keira's generous offer, she would imply that she hadn't Jude's best interests at heart.

She tried to imagine staying on in Alex's apartment while Keira set up camp on a stretcher in the living room. Keira would be constantly caring for Jude. Keira would always be there as a buffer between herself and Jude.

It was selfish of her to resent this, of course. She knew Jude should have the best possible medical supervision—and she'd known all along that her future with Jude was unclear at best.

If only he hadn't grasped her wrist and kissed her as she'd said goodbye. There'd been something so very intimate in the heat of his hand-grip and the brush of his lips, almost as if he'd been staking a claim. In front of Keira.

Walking away from him had been so painful.

But how much worse would it be to try to hang around like a fifth wheel, becoming more and more aware each day that she wasn't really wanted?

'You shouldn't have to camp on a stretcher,' she told Keira, covering her disappointment with a tremulous smile. 'I'll move my things out so you can be comfortable.'

The other woman frowned. 'But where will you go?'

Emily hesitated. She wasn't ready to go home to Wandabilla yet. 'I can stay on at my grand-mother's at Sunshine Beach.'

'The beach? Lucky you.' Keira couldn't quite hide the flash of triumph in her eyes. 'That's perfect then, isn't it?'

CHAPTER TEN

JUDE dropped his overnight bag in his bedroom, set his laptop on the desk, but left it unopened. His eyes were gradually improving, thank goodness, but it would be a while yet before he was reading a computer screen.

Just the same, he was relieved to be back in the apartment, the next best thing to his own home.

He went to the kitchen, which seemed strangely empty without Emily. Not that he thought of her as a 'kitchen' kind of woman, but they'd had some great times in here, just hanging out, preparing meals, eating, washing up.

As he continued on to the living room, he realised the whole damn apartment felt empty without Emily.

He wondered where Keira had got to. No doubt he should offer her tea or coffee before she headed off.

To his surprise, he heard noises coming from

Alex's bedroom. He headed down the hall, turning at the doorway, remembering the last time he'd been in this room. In bed with Emily.

Now, the white sheets that he and Emily had tangled in were in a heap on the floor, and Keira was smoothing a new navy-blue sheet over the king-size mattress.

'I didn't expect you to start on the laundry,' Jude said, surprised.

Keira shrugged and pulled a coy face. 'Call me fussy, but I like clean sheets.'

'*You* like them?' Jude frowned at her. 'I'm sorry. Have I missed something? You're not planning to stay here, are you?'

'Naturally, Jude. How else can I look after you?'

'I don't need looking after.'

'Don't be stubborn. Of course you do. You're just out of hospital.'

Jude scowled. How had he not seen this possibility? Why hadn't he guessed that Keira would be in her element when a man was in a weakened state?

He suppressed a sigh, which she might have interpreted as tiredness. 'I've been released from hospital because I'm fine, Keira. I've been told what to watch for. I have a phone if I need help. Apart from that, I can manage just as I always have. On my own.'

'But why put yourself to all that trouble when I'm perfectly willing to help?'

Jude knew there was no point in repeating the obvious—that he didn't need help. It would only lead to an argument and that was the last thing he wanted today.

Just the same, he didn't want Keira supervising his every move, taking his blood pressure half a dozen times a day, asking questions about his headaches or the colour of his urine, for crying out loud.

More to the point, if Keira was moving into *this* room, where would Emily sleep?

Jude's frown deepened. 'It's a bit rich of you to move in before I check with Emily.'

'Oh, that's not a problem. I sorted it with her.' Keira smiled at him as she stuffed a pillow into a navy-blue case.

'Sorted? How?'

'We had a nice little chat yesterday, at the hospital.'

That was quick work. Jude's temper stirred. Why hadn't he been included in this discussion?

Keira stuffed another pillow into its case and set it neatly on the bed.

Jude watched her with mounting irritation. 'I assumed you were dropping me off here and then heading on to Mount Tamborine.'

'Good heavens, no. I couldn't desert you, Jude. You're more important than my recreation.'

'Now hang on. I've already told you I don't need a nurse. I certainly don't need you to give up your precious leave from Afghanistan. You know the mountains clear your head and get you centred again.'

At any rate, that was the line Keira had always spun him.

Truth was, he didn't want her here now. He didn't want any woman fussing over him. That was why he'd sent Emily away. He needed to deal with this recovery on his own, and he didn't want to see anyone until he felt confident within himself that he was going to be OK.

Now, without warning, a wave of dizziness made him sway a little. He gripped the door-frame, hoping Keira didn't notice.

'Listen,' he told her, 'I don't want to be rude,

or to sound unappreciative of your efforts, but I'd like to have a little time on my own.'

The bed was made now and Keira was bundling up the dirty linen—the linen Jude and Emily had slept in. He wondered if she'd guessed.

'I think you're being very foolish, Jude. Stubborn and foolish. I'm sure Dr Stanley wouldn't approve.'

'First sign of a problem, I'll be in touch with Stanley.'

Keira stood clutching the sheets against her stomach, lips clamped together in a scowl. She was making it clear that she thought he was crazy. 'Are you certain?'

'Absolutely.'

'Then be it on your head,' she said in a tight, hurt voice and, letting the sheets drop to the floor, she pushed past him out of the room.

In the hallway, she whirled around to send him a parting scowl. 'There's something you should realise, Jude Marlowe. This need of yours to hide your imperfections is *not* a strength. It's a failing.'

Jude sighed. All he'd wanted was a little peace and quiet.

* * *

With an overnight bag in one hand and a heavy supermarket bag in the other, Emily climbed the stairs to the apartment.

She'd changed her mind about retreating to her grandmother's place and letting Keira Arnold take over caring for Jude, and she'd switched tack for two very good reasons. First—Jude, in his weakened state, might actually need shielding from Keira's bossiness. Second—staying away was wimpy, passive behaviour.

Emily was tired of being a loser in love.

Ever since her teens, she'd been hoping that love would fall into her lap, the way it had apparently done for her parents and her brother. Finally—and yes, finding the nerve to try that striptease had helped—she was beginning to understand that love wasn't a gift that arrived from above. It required a little risk-taking. Winning took courage.

She certainly needed courage now. Coming hot on the heels of her break-up, she hadn't wanted to believe she might be in love again so soon. But she loved Jude with a depth she'd never experienced before. She felt truly connected to him on so many levels.

Just two weeks with him had shown her how totally superficial her previous relationships had been. Now she believed she could be best mates with Jude as well as his lover. It was exactly the kind of relationship her parents had, and it was too special to let slip away.

This time she was determined to win.

She straightened her shoulders as she reached the top of the steps, but had to take a step back when the apartment's door flew open and a women's figure stormed out, letting the door slam behind her.

Keira Arnold glared at Emily. 'What are you doing here?'

Emily's stomach clenched. 'I changed my mind.' It sounded hopelessly lame. Not a good start. She held up the supermarket bag. 'I'll take care of the cooking. It's not exactly Jude's forte.'

'Jude's forte is pigheadedness,' Keira spat. 'Watch out.'

Then she rushed down the steps, pushing past Emily so roughly that her large shoulder bag banged against her, knocking the shopping bag to the floor. Apples spilled from the bag and bounced down the concrete steps. A packet split, seeping white flour.

'Bloody hell,' groaned Keira.

She didn't apologise, but she did chase after the apples and dump them into the bag, while Emily did her best to seal up the flour packet.

'They're not too bruised,' Keira said, referring to the apples. She cocked her head towards the door. 'Good luck in there, but I don't like your chances.'

Open-mouthed with surprise, Emily watched as she hurried down the steps and disappeared into the car park.

Shaken, she set the shopping down while she extracted the spare key she'd kept, then opened the door and let herself inside.

'Hello, Jude?' she called softly, standing in the hallway, clutching her bags.

It was several moments before he appeared at the doorway to his room. Just the sight of him set small flames inside Emily, but she could see that behind his sunglasses he was scowling as fiercely as Keira.

'What are you doing here?' he demanded.

Not quite the greeting she'd hoped for. He sounded tired. Fed up. Angry.

'I brought some groceries.' She was almost apologetic.

Jude sighed, rubbing at his forehead.

'You look tired,' she said, knowing she probably sounded as worried as she suddenly felt. Why had Keira left? Wasn't she supposed to be supervising Jude's post-operative care?

'Please, go and rest,' she said. 'I'll just pop these things in the kitchen. I won't disturb you.'

Jude didn't bother with thanks. He gave a slight nod, then shut his door.

Emily gulped. Just as well she hadn't expected this to be easy.

Jude lay with the curtains drawn and his eyes closed. He'd been drained by the argument with Keira, and he simply had no energy to deal with Emily as well.

He'd almost wept when he'd seen her, standing in the hallway looking like a Renaissance angel with her arms full of twenty-first century groceries.

But she shouldn't have come. He hated her

seeing him like this. He'd tried to keep her at a distance, but she'd come to the hospital anyhow and it had nearly killed him to see her yesterday, sitting on the far side of the room like any run-of-the-mill visitor.

What was he going to do about her?

Was he in love with her?

He'd never felt this intensity of confusion and distraction over any other woman. He'd never felt so lonely as when he was apart from her. He'd never spent hours reliving every memory of the way a woman moved or smiled. He'd never felt so incomplete in a woman's absence.

But, in his current state, a future with Emily seemed too much to hope for.

His sister, Charlotte, thought otherwise. She'd told him so this morning when she'd said goodbye before retuning to Sydney.

'Hang on to this one,' she'd said, hugging him with tears in her eyes. 'Don't push Emily away, Jude. I know she's right for you.'

'How can you know?' He was desperate to hear her answer.

'Don't be a deadbeat,' she'd gently chided. 'You're my brother. I know these things. I've known you all my life, and I've met most of your girlfriends, and I—'

Charlotte had given a shrugging little laugh. 'OK, maybe it's only a hunch, and I don't know where the hunch comes from. Call it sisterly intuition or wishful thinking, but there's something about Emily that feels very in tune with you, Jude.'

In tune. In harmony.

It was such a simplistic concept, but Charlotte had hit straight on the truth. When Jude remembered everything he and Emily had shared together, from watching movies to breakfast in bed, there'd been many, many harmonious moments and next to no discord.

That in itself was interesting. He usually ended up arguing with his girlfriends, or disappointing them, just as his father had argued with or disappointed his mother. Jude had assumed that he'd inherited the failing.

Perhaps he was reading too much into his sister's comments, but he couldn't deny that he'd loved having Emily in his life. *Loved?* There ought to be a stronger word. The thought that he might lose her horrified him. But after the disappointments she'd had with boyfriends, he had no intention of offering her false hope.

Until his vision cleared and his headaches eased, he had nothing to offer her except uncertainty and poorly suppressed fears.

She deserved so much more.

At the very least she deserved a whole man.

Jude grimaced as Keira's final accusation pounded in his head. Was she right? Was his need to hide his imperfections a failing rather than a strength?

Probably.

But his desire to keep his weaknesses hidden was so ingrained that he couldn't imagine living any other way. He'd learned as a child to cope on his own and to paper over any visible cracks in the image he presented to the world.

This warped version of coping probably came from having parents who arrived home every night, tired from the Court House and preferring to drink expensive wine and to argue with each other than to take more than a cursory interest in their children. Jude had spent many evenings entertaining Charlotte with bedtime stories. It was how he'd discovered and nurtured his writing talent.

Their nanny had been kindness personified and Jude had adored her but, under his father's watchful eye, even she had been instructed to offer minimum pampering when the children were sick or hurt.

Charlotte had reacted quite differently to their upbringing. She'd taken up nursing and thrown herself into caring for others. After she'd married, she'd become a perfect wife and mother, devoted to her family.

Jude had chosen fierce independence. He could totally lose himself in his writing, so he'd been more or less happy with his life as a semi-recluse. Before Emily.

Could he change? Or was he fooling himself to think he might ever be right for her, even if he was fully recovered?

The question was too hard to answer, certainly now…when his head was aching and he needed to sleep…

Jude slept for hours, and Emily couldn't believe how disconcerting she found this. She almost wished Keira was still there so that she could check if this lengthy sleep was normal.

She was as nervous as a mother with a brand-new baby. Twice she crept to the door of Jude's room and opened it a crack just to see if his chest was still rising and falling.

The rest of the time, she kept herself busy in the kitchen, making a beef casserole and a batch of muffins, as well as a proper homemade chicken soup with vegetables and barley. Clearly, Jude's illness brought out the homebody in her.

It was dark when he finally woke. He came into the kitchen, tousle-haired and barefoot, with a hand shading his eyes.

Quickly, Emily turned the overhead light off. 'Sorry.' Now there was just a soft light coming from the pantry. 'Is that better?'

'Thanks, that's fine.'

'How are you feeling?'

'Fabulous. I really needed that sleep. Could never get enough in the hospital.' He shot a frowning glance to the stove. 'You've been busy.'

'I thought you might like a bit more than tinned soup.'

His mouth tilted, not quite cracking a smile.

He was wearing a long-sleeved grey T-shirt and jeans and the light from the pantry cast chiaroscuro shadows, highlighting the masculine planes and angles of his face. Despite the dark stubble on his jaw, he looked a little pale, but Emily was quite sure no one had ever looked more lovable.

She wanted to go to him, to slip her arms around him, to press her cheek against his chest, her ear against his heart.

Alternatively, she wouldn't have objected if he wanted to put his arms around her just as he had when she'd been standing at the sink on the day before the operation.

Neither of them moved, however.

'Are you hungry?' she asked.

Jude rubbed a hand over his stomach. 'Starving.'

'There's a beef casserole or there's chicken soup.'

'That's very kind of you, Emily.' His darkly lashed eyes glinted silver in the soft light and he sent her a sad smile. 'I'm really grateful for the food.'

'No problem,' she said uncertainly, sensing

that he was about to say something more, something she didn't want to hear.

Jude looked uncomfortable. 'You weren't actually planning on staying here, were you?'

Fear tightened like an icy fist in her chest. 'Don't...' Oh, God, she couldn't believe she was asking this. 'Don't you want me to stay?'

At Jude's hesitation, her insides shrank.

With a pained grimace, he rubbed at his unshaven jaw. 'Look, I know this is your cousin's place.' His gaze flickered, not quite meeting hers. 'But could you give me a little space for a few more days?'

'How many days?'

'Till next week?'

Next week?

Dismayed, Emily grabbed hold of a bench top for support. Jude had told her he was feeling fine, and he'd sent Keira packing. Didn't that leave the door open for her to come back?

'I'm just not ready to be sociable,' he said.

'I wouldn't expect you to be sociable. But I wanted to help.'

'Thanks, but I don't need help.'

He said this with some reluctance, but that couldn't soften the blow.

He didn't want her.

She'd been so carried away, rushing here with her dreams of courage and winning. But her silly dream had been one-sided, based on a foolish hope that Jude and she might—

Oh, good grief, she was an idiot.

How had this happened again? How had she fooled herself into believing that this man was different, that this time she really was going to make a success of a very special relationship?

The kitchen blurred before Emily's eyes. Her throat ached horribly.

'I'm sorry, Jude,' she said in a voice that sounded way too tight and scared. 'I thought… I assumed…'

She couldn't finish. Not without breaking down and making a fool of herself. Not without losing the last tattered shreds of her dignity.

'I'll get my things,' she said instead.

Blinded by tears, she hurried from the kitchen. She hadn't unpacked her bag. It was still standing just inside the door to Alex's room, so it was a simple matter to grab it.

Jude was in the hallway, looking way too tall and gorgeous and grim. 'You do understand?' he said.

No, she didn't understand at all. But she sure as hell wasn't going to stand here and listen to his explanation of why her presence was suddenly a problem for him—

After everything they'd shared together.

She didn't want to hear his version of their relationship. She knew how it would go—that they'd had a brief pre-surgery fling with no promises.

'You don't mind staying at Sunshine Beach till next week?' he asked.

Emily didn't answer at first. She *did* mind and she wanted to tell him so. Loudly. If he wasn't still recovering, she might have.

'I may not need to come,' she said tightly. 'Not if you are coping just fine on your own. I'll have to see how I'm placed next week.' She opened the door. 'Oh, and I've left your car in the garage. Thanks for the loan.'

'Emily.'

Chin high, Emily refused to turn back. She couldn't bear to prolong the pain, knowing the result was inevitable. Marching through the doorway, she didn't copy Keira and let the door slam behind her, even though she now felt huge sympathy for the other woman. Clearly they were both Jude's victims.

To her immense relief, she was able to hail a taxi as soon as she reached the footpath. Clambering in, she sat hunched in the back, wrapped in a pain that was all too familiar.

She was such a fool. Jude had actually rescued her from this kind of hurting over Michael, and yet…once again…she'd fooled herself into thinking that she was safe to fall in love one more time.

It didn't help that she understood why Jude was doing this—that he was so much the he-man he hated having anyone see him in a weakened state. That attitude didn't really make sense when she'd already been living with him and she'd seen him laid low by headaches.

At least she was certain about one thing—this was the last time she'd push her way into Jude's life. She'd gone to his mountain home at Alex's request, even though she'd known she wasn't really welcome. She'd gone to the hospital against

Jude's wishes, and she'd come here this afternoon instead of waiting for him to invite her.

Three strikes and she was out.

Finally, she'd got the message.

Jude's reserve had all the hallmarks of a sinking relationship. She'd been on the receiving end
of enough rejections and disappointments to recognise the warning signs.

Why hadn't she seen this coming?

*Jude made no promises. I knew that, and yet
I still fooled myself.*

Somehow—some-*crazy*-how—she'd managed
to trick herself into believing that this time with
Jude had been different. This time she'd experienced a truer connection, a *two-way* connection. She and Jude had understood each other
and together they'd helped each other through
difficulties.

Jude had consoled her about Michael, and
she'd tried to distract him during the lead-in to
his surgery. There'd been a balance of give and
take. They'd been a team.

A temporary team, apparently.

Oh, God. She'd promised herself this wouldn't
happen again. She should have known. Unlike

Michael, Jude had at least warned her. *No promises*. One thing she could say about Jude, he hadn't deceived her.

She'd done that entirely on her own.

I've left your car in the garage. Thanks for the loan.

Emily's last words had been delivered so coldly. Jude couldn't believe the pain they'd caused him, worse than any physical discomfort.

He'd totally stuffed up. He was a gold-plated fool. He'd convinced himself that he was asking her to leave for her own good. After all, a recovering patient wasn't very good company for a beautiful, vital young woman. But he hadn't meant to hurt her feelings, or to make her feel rejected.

In his weakened state, he couldn't run after her, damn it, but he was desperate to make amends. He grabbed his phone and pressed her number, but his call went straight to her message bank. No doubt she'd turned her phone off.

She was mad with him. No question.

Angry at his stupidity, Jude almost hurled the phone across the room. He couldn't believe he'd been so hung up about his damn eyesight that he hadn't taken any time to consider Emily's perspective.

Perhaps the surgeon had removed his entire brain?

It was just as well he'd slept all afternoon because sleep eluded him for most of the night.

In the morning, on the dot of seven-thirty, Jude tried Emily's phone again, with the same result—her voice asked him to please leave a message.

Emily, it's Jude. Please ring back.

He ate breakfast—baked beans, unheated, straight from the can—then he tried Emily's phone again. He tried twice more during the day, but pride prevented him from leaving a string of pleading messages. He wasn't going to explain or apologise to a machine. He wanted to speak to Emily.

By evening, he still couldn't get through.

OK, so he'd proved spectacularly that he was a thickhead—but even he could work out that Emily was deliberately *not* answering his calls.

He heated some of her chicken soup. It was

delicious but each mouthful reminded him of
his stupidity. In the living room he turned on
the CD player. Not wanting to bother his eyes
with a new selection, he let the machine replay
the last disc inserted.

It filled the room with a slow, sultry beat.

His heart thudded.

From now until forever he would never hear
this music without thinking of Emily.

From the first deep throb of the double bass he
was remembering the little high kick she'd given
as she came into this room wearing a scrap of
copper silk and long black stockings.

In spite of everything, Jude smiled at the memory—smiled so hard that he was damn near
fighting tears, all too aware of the Emily-sized
hole in his life.

Having learned his lesson, Jude didn't call Emily
again till the end of the week and, during that
time, his body performed exactly as the surgeon
had predicted. His headaches eased and then
disappeared completely, and his vision gradually cleared. At his post-op check-up, he felt as

well as he ever had, and the only hurdle ahead of him now was an MRI in five weeks' time.

This news was too good not to share, but when he tried Emily's phone again, she still didn't answer.

More distressed than he could have believed, he gave in and dialled Granny Silver's number.

'Oh, Jude,' she said brightly. 'How are you?'

'Very well, thanks.'

'That is good news. I'm so pleased.'

'I was hoping to speak to Emily.'

'I'm sorry, Jude. Emily's not here. She's gone home to Wandabilla. She left three days ago.'

'Three days?' He almost choked on his disappointment. 'What happened? Was there a problem at the office?'

'More or less,' Granny Silver said evasively.

Jude waited for her to expand on this unsatisfactory situation, but there was silence on the other end of the line. 'Granny, is there anything else you can tell me?'

'I don't think so, Jude. Emily decided that it made sense for her to go home now. She wanted time to get a few things for her new business sorted before she was due back at the bank.'

Her new business.

She'd been excited about it at the hospital, but he'd been so caught up in his own sorry mess that he hadn't given her a chance to explain her ideas.

Granny sighed. 'I'm sorry, Jude. I don't think I can tell you any more than that. I know that Emily really appreciated your company in Brisbane and she enjoyed getting to know you. We've been keeping you in our thoughts, and we're hoping for a full recovery.'

'Thanks,' he said grimly.

There was a sound, as if she was about to say something else, and Jude tensed. Right now, he would take anything, even a lecture from an octogenarian on the foolishness of his ways. Anything that would help him to heal the yawning gulf that separated him from Emily.

'I believe you're finishing a book,' Granny said. 'I hope that goes well.'

The book? He couldn't care less about the book. Not now. Not when his perfect girl had slipped away from him. Not when she'd flown out of his life with the same speed she'd escaped that Michael character. Clearly she'd placed him in the same league as the rat.

Jude was still grappling with shock and struggling to find words when Granny said, 'Have you heard that Alex is staying overseas for a few more weeks? I believe he's picked up several international clients. Isn't that wonderful? It means you'll be on your own for a few more weeks. I expect you'll enjoy the privacy.'

Emily had been coaching her grandmother. No doubt about that.

CHAPTER ELEVEN

WANDABILLA was a typical Queensland country town with wide streets edged with old-fashioned shops and offices, and a strip of well tended garden down the middle. Jude parked his vehicle outside the bank where Emily was manager.

In the six weeks since she'd returned here, he'd walked a tightrope. He'd desperately needed to see her, to explain and to make amends, but his instincts had urged him to hold back till he'd had the final all clear and everything was in place. He'd gone with his instincts and now, at last, he had all his ducks in a row.

Just the same, chances were this reunion would be tough. But he was ready.

He tested the knot in the tie he'd teamed with a sports jacket, cream moleskins and a blue chambray shirt. No point in looking too citified.

Now, as he stepped onto the footpath, he tried to ignore the band of tension that tightened around his chest. He pushed open the bank's old-fashioned swing doors.

'Good morning. I'd like to see the manager,' he told the girl at the front desk. 'I'm sorry about the short notice. I'm just passing through and it's urgent.'

The girl let her gaze linger, clearly checking him out, before she turned to her computer screen and scrolled down a page. 'Your name, sir?'

Jude hesitated, and prayed that Emily wouldn't refuse to see him.

'Jude Marlowe,' he said.

The girl looked up with a beaming smile. 'If you'll take a seat, Mr Simpson will be with you shortly.'

'Mr Simpson?' Jude stared at her, stunned. 'But I want to see the manager, Emily Silver.'

Without even checking her computer, the girl shook her head. 'Sorry, sir. Emily Silver doesn't work here.'

This was crazy. Jude had researched on the Internet, and he was sure he had the right bank. He'd even double-checked with Alex. Emily hadn't returned his calls, so this was his only option. He *had* to see her.

'There has to be a mistake. I know she works here.' Jude reached for his tie, wishing he could loosen the knot. He was choking in the damn thing.

'I'm sorry,' the girl said again. 'I should have been clearer. Emily Silver doesn't work here any more.'

Jude felt as if he'd run smack into an invisible glass wall. 'Has she been transferred?'

'No, she resigned.' The girl looked up at him from beneath mascara-thickened lashes. 'It was a big shock to everyone. Emily left a fortnight ago. Left the bank and left town.'

'I see.' Jude spoke calmly despite his rising panic. 'I'm sure she left a forwarding address.'

Once again, the girl shook her head. 'I have no authority to hand out personal information.'

Of course. He knew that. He'd been desperate, clutching at straws.

'Thank you,' he said, even though he was anything but grateful.

Turning on his heel, he strode out of the building into sunshine and a blank wall of fear.

* * *

Saturday mornings in the city were very different from Saturdays in Wandabilla. Emily sat at a café table on a footpath crowded with small tables, drinking coffee and reading the weekend papers. All around her, people were doing the same thing—drinking coffee, eating breakfast, reading alone or chatting in groups.

No one paid Emily the slightest attention, and she couldn't recognise a single face. How wonderful was that? After years of living in a tiny country town where she knew everyone and everyone knew her, plus every single detail of her private life, this urban anonymity was bliss.

She'd been living in Brisbane for a month now, renting a flat in Red Hill. In that time she'd thrown herself into starting up her fledgling business—a sun-safe fashion line for mothers and children. Sports shirts with long sleeves, casual tops, hats made from cottons that breathe, but sturdy enough to run about and play in.

She'd been struck by the idea while staying at Sunshine Beach. As a redhead, she'd always had to cover up in the outdoors, and in her childhood especially she'd found it such a bore. These days, it wasn't just an issue for people with really fair skin. Everyone was more conscious of sun protection and, with so many 'yummy mummies' enjoying an active outdoor life, Emily was sure her idea was a winner.

There was a lot to do. She'd teamed with a talented young designer who was actually the granddaughter of one of Granny Silver's friends, and the garments were being made by a cooperative of farmer's wives from Wandabilla. They'd been looking for a project that allowed them to work from home, and they'd leapt at Emily's idea. She was offering them very fair rates, of course.

Now she was also busy with marketing—sourcing a logo, organising a registered trade name, setting up a website.

Fortunately, she had enough savings and investments to see her through this early establishment phase, and she was quietly confident that this business was going to fly.

It was all very satisfying.

A waitress arrived with her breakfast—mushrooms on ciabatta bread. *Yum.* She folded her newspaper, keeping only the real-estate pages

open to peruse while she ate. She'd been toy-
ing with the idea of buying a house of her own.

With the flexibility of an Internet business,
she could more or less live wherever she liked.
The world was now her oyster, but she rather
liked Brisbane and being close to both Alex and
Granny.

Emily cut a piece of toast and topped it with
dark, succulent, peppery mushrooms, munching happily as she scanned the rows of photos.

She wasn't quite sure what kind of place she
would prefer—a slick modern apartment or a
cute cottage with a leafy garden. It would be
rather nice if something leapt out at her, a kind
of real-estate love at first sight, but she was in
no hurry to buy. She turned a page, helping herself to more mushrooms.

Then she saw it.

Halfway down the page.

A photo she instantly recognised that made
her go cold all over and caused a piece of toast
to stick in her throat.

A distinctively beautiful home made of timber
and glass with a wonderful view of rainforest-
clad hillsides. Emily checked the address—

Mount Tamborine—and her heart crashed against her ribcage.

It had to be Jude's house. Of course it was his. It was highly unlikely that another home on Tamborine Mountain would be built to exactly that same design. Besides, she could see the brick-paved driveway where she'd parked the hire car and the flat rock stepping stones that led to Jude's front door.

There could be no doubt. Jude's gorgeous home was for sale. Emily clapped a hand over her mouth to stop herself from crying out loud.

How could Jude sell the place he loved so much? Why would he?

He'd told her once that he would be prepared to give up his mountain home and lifestyle if he found the right woman. Surely he hadn't found his perfect someone in the few weeks since his operation?

What else could this mean? Had he returned to one of his previous girlfriends?

It was unlikely, Emily decided, given all the messages on her phone that she'd ignored.

What else might have prompted this sale? Financial difficulties were a possibility, but somehow Emily didn't think that was Jude's problem.

Had his eyes deteriorated? Could he no longer risk living in such an isolated home?

Much as she hated this thought, it was surely the most likely explanation. Even though Granny Silver had reported that Jude had rung and said his vision was fine, something must have gone wrong since then. Some kind of relapse.

And if the worst had happened, he probably couldn't stand to live there surrounded by a view he couldn't see.

The thought was almost too sad to bear.

Emily had tried so hard to focus on enjoying her post-Jude life and put him out of her thoughts. But her avoidance of him had been based on the assumption that he was fine.

Now, any possibility of remaining aloof from Jude had been wiped out by one photo.

Abandoning her breakfast, she snatched up the page with the picture of his house, folded it swiftly and stuffed it into her shoulder bag.

'How was your meal?' the girl at the cash register enquired.

'It was delicious,' Emily assured her. 'I'm

sorry I couldn't stay to finish it. There's been an emergency.'

The girl sent Emily a look of sympathy as she rushed away. She was halfway down the footpath before she came to a skidding halt, realising she had no idea where she was running to. She'd taken off in a blind panic.

Now, as she came to her senses, she pulled her phone from her bag and keyed in Alex's number.

'Jude's selling his house,' she told her cousin the instant he answered. 'Do you know why? Is something wrong? Is there a problem with his eyes?'

'Hey, calm down,' Alex soothed. 'One question at a time. What's this about Jude's house?'

'It's for sale. I've just seen the ad in this morning's paper.'

'Really? Are you sure it's Jude's house?'

'Positive. I can't believe it, Alex.'

'I haven't heard anything about it but, to be honest, I think Jude's avoiding me. He hasn't answered my phone calls or my emails. I'm assuming that's because he's way overdue with delivering his latest manuscript.'

'Is he?' This news only deepened Emily's

fears. Jude had been close to finishing the book weeks ago. 'I thought his eyesight was OK.'

'So did I. There was no mention of a problem last time we spoke, but that was quite a few weeks back. Now you've got me worried. I'll try calling him again.'

'Thanks. So will I.'

But Emily didn't ring Jude straight away. After she ended the call to Alex, she slid the phone into her pocket and started walking back up the steep hill to her flat. She hoped the long climb would help her to stop panicking. She needed a chance to think about this situation with a clear head.

The ad in the paper said that Jude's house was to be auctioned on Wednesday and the property was open for inspection over this weekend. This meant that potential buyers could be traipsing through that beautiful house right at this moment. They would be falling in love with its hilltop location, with its stunning views and its distinctive and elegant architecture.

Anyone who stepped through the doorway to Jude's house was bound to fall in love and want to buy it.

But Jude loved the house, too, just as he loved his mountains and hiking the skyline and watching the weather roll in over Sunset Ridge.

How could he bear to let all that go?

Emily wanted to ring him. Desperately.

But what did a girl say to a man after two months of silence, after she'd taken off with very little explanation and refused to return his calls?

I'm sorry. I was saving my sanity.

I was trying to be tough.

It was all about survival.

She'd retreated, afraid that she'd read too much into that wondrous short time she'd lived with Jude, and knowing she was a relationship dunce.

But how did her hang-ups about her relationships stack up against Jude's serious problems—losing his eyesight and losing his beautiful home?

A major thing holding her back was the fact that she'd already been way too pushy with Jude in the past. Heavens, the only reason she'd met him in the first place was because she'd turned up on the poor man's doorstep, completely out of the blue.

That had just been the start. She'd gone to the

mountains, she'd done that fateful striptease and, after his surgery, she'd come back to the apartment too soon. Now she cringed at the thought of yet again pushing her way uninvited into Jude's life. Hadn't she given up that right when she ran away?

Her phone sat on her kitchen table all weekend while she circled it, thinking about Jude, worrying about Jude and missing him so badly she felt sick.

Alex didn't ring back, so he probably hadn't got through to Jude, either, but on Monday Emily was very tempted to rush over to Alex's place and tell him the whole sorry story of her brief relationship with his client.

Like old times, they could open a bottle of wine and she'd pour out her troubles, and Alex would be sympathetic, and she'd feel better...

Except...

Except...she wouldn't feel better, would she?

Not this time. Not about Jude.

Besides, she didn't want to tell Alex about watching herons and sunsets with Jude. There were some memories that felt too precious to share. She certainly wouldn't tell her cousin about her attempted striptease…or the night that had followed.

Instead, Emily threw herself into a cleaning frenzy, vacuuming, mopping and polishing until her tiny flat shone. She spent the afternoon fiddling with her new website.

On Tuesday, a parcel arrived from Wandabilla—the first sample collection of sun-safe shirts and caps. They were just beautiful and Emily was thrilled, but she would have been more thrilled if she hadn't been so distracted.

In less than twenty-four hours Jude's house would go under the auctioneer's hammer. She still didn't know why, but she was sure the reason had to be desperate and she couldn't bear to think of Jude going through such an ordeal alone.

Shouldn't she be there, too?

The realisation dawned on her like a slow, warming sunrise.

Even if Jude had problems with his eyes, he would almost certainly be at the auction—and she could be there, in the background. She wouldn't be pushy. She wouldn't make her presence obvious. She would blend in with the crowd, keep an eye on Jude from a distance, be circumspect. If she sensed that he needed her help in any way, she would be ready. On call. To step in as a friend. She would make sure Jude understood that she wasn't barging back into his life.

Emily went to bed happy. She had a plan.

CHAPTER TWELVE

THE large number of cars parked along the edges of the winding mountain road didn't surprise Emily. She'd guessed that Jude's house would be popular. Just the same, she felt sick knowing that in an hour or two, someone else would own his beloved retreat.

It was cool in the mountains so she pulled a denim jacket over her T-shirt, making a quick check of her reflection in the rear-vision mirror. She'd dressed casually and kept her make-up subtle, aiming to blend into the crowd—but she was sadly aware that none of this was necessary if Jude couldn't see her.

She gave a little shake, needing to banish such thoughts. *No tears now.* Locking the car door, she set off, chin high, determined to be brave. And circumspect.

An assortment of people had gathered in the driveway—businessmen in suits, several couples of retirement age, a few people who looked like hiking types, lean and slightly weather-beaten.

Many of these people were probably hoping to buy their dream home today, and the auctioneer was on the move, smiling and chatting, no doubt trying to suss out the genuine bidders.

Emily's stomach fluttered nervously. She didn't care at all when heads turned to stare at her curiously. She just wished she knew where Jude was and how he was feeling right now.

The auction, they were told, was to be held on the back deck, and everyone filed up the external timber stairway. Emily held her breath as she followed the crowd. On the deck, she melted to the back of the group, shocked by how dreadfully anxious she felt—anxious for Jude.

Over the past weeks, she'd been trying to keep her thoughts Jude-free but, from the moment she'd seen the house in the paper, she'd been learning all over again how very deeply she cared for him, and now she was flooded by a host of feelings that she'd tried for two months to suppress.

She loved him.

There was no escaping it.

It didn't matter where Jude lived or whether or not he could see, she was still in love with him. Weeks of separation hadn't changed that. Nothing would change it. She would probably go to her grave knowing that he was The One.

But if Jude's circumstances were even worse than they'd been two months ago, he would almost certainly push her away again.

Still, she had to hope there was some way she could help.

The auctioneer opened the large timber-framed glass door that led into the house and spoke to someone inside. Emily's heart picked up pace. He was probably asking Jude to come out.

Despite the chatter of the people all around her, she was sure she could hear a firm tread on the floorboards inside the house. Then she saw a familiar figure in the doorway—tall, dark-haired, broad-shouldered—Jude, sexier than ever in a dark blue shirt and jeans.

Her heart thudded painfully. Seeing him again brought such a crush of memories…his smile, his conversation, his kisses, his touch… She'd missed him during every second of her self-imposed isolation.

And then she realised something else.

Jude didn't seem to have a problem with his sight. He wasn't wearing dark glasses and there was no hesitancy in his movements, nothing careful about the way he strolled onto the deck, hands sunk casually in the pockets of his jeans. He smiled and nodded to a couple of the men in suits, shook their hands, waved to someone else at the back of the crowd.

It was quite obvious that he could see, and Emily's first reaction was a rush of brilliant, over-the-moon euphoria.

But this was quickly followed by confusion. If he was OK, why was he selling his house? Had he found Miss Right, after all?

Then Jude froze.

Across the crowd, his gaze locked with Emily's, and shock registered as he stared at her.

She wanted to smile, but she hadn't a chance. She couldn't move a muscle. She'd turned to stone.

Without a word or a gesture to anyone, Jude crossed the deck towards her. People moved out of the way, making room for him as if they sensed a man on a mission.

In no time he was standing directly in front of Emily, his grey eyes burning. 'What are you doing here?'

'I...' Her mouth was so dry she had to run her tongue over her lips and try again. 'I was hoping to see you.'

He gave a helpless, stunned shake of his head, and then he gripped her arm. 'Come with me.'

He grasped her tightly and she was aware of the force of his tension as he steered her across the deck while curious eyes followed them.

As soon as they were inside the house, Jude released her. Then he stood back, running a shaking hand through his hair. 'I can't quite believe this.'

'It must be a...a surprise,' Emily admitted and she swallowed nervously. 'You look well, Jude.'

'I'm very well, thank you—apart from shell-shock.'

Now she could see that he did look a bit dazed.

'What are you doing here?' he asked again.

'I saw the for sale ad in the paper and I had to come.'

For painful seconds he stared at her and his

eyes reflected a breathtaking mix of emotions. 'Why, Emily? Why did you have to come?'

'So many reasons.' Now her heart was going crazy. She could scarcely breathe. 'Some you might not believe.'

'Try me.'

Oh, help. Emily hadn't expected to reach this moment so quickly. She'd rehearsed all kinds of explanations, but now, with Jude standing so stiffly before her, watching her so intently and fiercely, the answers flew out of her head.

She had no choice. She had to give him the only excuse she could think of—

'I was desperately worried about you.'

Jude looked unconvinced.

'I just had to see that you were OK, Jude. I couldn't think why you were selling this house, unless something had gone wrong with your eyes.'

'My eyes are fine.'

Now she couldn't bring herself to add the other reason, that she feared he might have found the perfect woman and that he was giving up this lifestyle to be with her.

The pain of that possibility was too much.

'Why have you come here after all this time?' Jude asked her again.

There was only one true reason. 'I'm…I'm in love with you.'

Oh, good grief. Had she really said it aloud?

'I'm sorry, Jude. I know that's the last thing you wanted to hear.'

His eyes were glistening now, and his throat worked as if he found it painful to swallow. He shot a quick glance out to the deck, where several people were peering in through the glass door.

'We need privacy,' he said, turning his back on the crowd and nodding to a door leading off the living room.

Emily frowned. 'What…about the auction?'

'This is more important.'

Her heart was trembling as she followed him into his study. She was aware of thick carpet beneath her feet, walls lined with crowded bookshelves, a computer and a scattering of pens and paper on a large silky oak desk. She was also nervously aware that she'd once again barged back into Jude's life—this time with the ultimate intrusion—a declaration of love.

Jude closed the door, then turned to her. There was no window in this room and they were completely alone, and she wondered if he was going to tell her off for interfering and then send her packing.

He stood tall in the middle of the carpeted floor, took a deep breath and folded his arms across his considerable chest. 'Did you know I've been to Wandabilla looking for you?'

Emily felt her knees shake with shock.

'When?' she asked, unable to wipe the disbelief from her voice.

'A couple of weeks back, after you'd already left town.' Jude eased back against his desk. 'I planned to come looking for you again, just as soon as I had this sorted.'

'Had what sorted? Selling the house?'

He nodded.

'But I don't understand. Why do you want to sell this place? It doesn't make sense. I thought you loved living here.'

'I have loved it,' he said simply.

She gave a helpless flap of her hands. 'Then why sell? Your eyes are fine, aren't they?'

'Absolutely. I've been very lucky. At the six week MRI, I scored a clean bill of health.'

'That's wonderful news.' It was such good news and she wanted to rush to him, to wrap him in a joyous bear hug. But she didn't dare, of course. Not after his grim reaction to her embarrassing, poorly timed confession of love.

'I'm even more confused now,' she said instead. 'Forgive me for speaking like a bank manager, but I do understand that finances are very tight for everyone at the moment.'

'I don't have a problem with my finances,' Jude said.

As if on cue, the auctioneer's raised voice reached them from outside. He was giving his introductory spiel.

'Don't you need to be out there?' Emily asked.

Jude shook his head. 'As I said, this conversation is more important. I'd like to explain to you why I'm selling the house.'

Something in his voice and in his eyes made her feel as if he was leading her to the very brink of a precipice.

A wave of dizziness overcame her, and for a

terrible moment she thought she was going to faint. 'You've found her.'

'Excuse me?'

Oh, help. This was so painful. Why couldn't he just tell her instead of dragging this out? 'You told me you'd give up this house for the right woman. I'm guessing you must have found her.'

Outside, the auctioneer's voice grew louder and more excited. The bidding must have started, but Jude didn't seem the slightest bit interested.

His eyes were lit by a funny-sad smile. Directed at her. 'Yes, I've found her,' he said gently.

'That's—' Emily tried to form the word *wonderful*, but her lips were too wobbly.

'Emily, can't you guess?'

No, she was too scared to think. Her heartbeats were pounding too loudly, thundering in her ears. She shook her head. Tears threatened.

In one stride Jude was beside her and his arms were around her, supporting her, holding her against the strong, safe wall of his chest. He pressed his face into her hair and then he kissed her brow, her cheek, her chin. 'Emily.'

For a moment she was too stunned to think. Then she pulled back with a gasp.

Jude's smile was lighting his eyes and making the skin at their edges crinkle. 'You're more important to me than anything.'

'But you're not selling this house because of me, Jude?' Her heart stumbled, picked itself up and did a cartwheel. 'That's crazy.'

'No, selling my house isn't crazy. The crazy thing was letting you go.' With his thumb, Jude traced a soft line down the curve of her cheek. 'The crazy thing was being too afraid to admit that I loved you.'

His smile made her want to cry for all the right reasons. 'That's why I went to Wandabilla and it's why I was gearing up to cross oceans or slay dragons. I was going to find you, my dear, sweet girl, to tell you that I love you. I love you so much.'

He said this as if loving her changed everything.

As if nothing else in the entire universe mattered.

'Being with you is more important than where

I live. I wouldn't want to live here without you. I was planning to start over somewhere else if I couldn't find you.'

He reached for her hands. 'I told you I could give up this house for the right girl. And I meant it. You're the right girl, Emily. The only girl.'

It wasn't easy to tell a man he was hopelessly crazy and kiss him at the same time, but Emily did her best, with her arms wrapped around his neck, with her body pressed close to his hunky muscles, and with tears streaming down her face.

She might have gone on kissing him for ever if there hadn't been a pressing question she needed to ask.

As she reluctantly pulled back, she could hear the auctioneer's voice outside growing increasingly more persuasive and agitated.

'Jude,' she said with sudden urgency, 'what if *I* don't want you to lose your house?'

She saw a flash in his eyes—and she had her answer. Now there wasn't a moment to lose.

She tugged at his hand. 'Come on. We've got to hurry.'

Thinking more clearly, she dropped his hand, and began to run ahead of him. 'Correction, *I've* got to hurry.'

Another sunset...

'This calls for bubbles,' Jude said as he carried a bottle of chilled champagne and two flutes onto the deck.

The auctioneer and potential buyers had left now, and the two of them were alone. Emily was leaning against the deck's railing, enjoying the view. She turned and grinned at him. Her hair gleamed like autumn leaves against the spring green of the rainforest, and he thought how perfectly relaxed and happy she looked in this setting, so different from the cool and collected professional who'd so competently joined in the bidding on his house.

Then again, he should have guessed that Emily's career as a country bank manager enabled her to morph into an auction genius.

He worked the champagne cork free and it gave a soft pop. The wine sparkled and fizzed as he filled their glasses and he handed one to Emily. 'Congratulations to the new home owner.'

'Thank you, sir.' She touched her glass to his. 'Here's to us.'

He stood for a moment, smiling a little dazedly into her eyes, sipping his drink as he came to terms with everything that had happened in the past hour.

His world had taken a three-sixty degree spin.

And here he was…celebrating.

He was a lucky man.

Un-flaming-believably lucky.

Emily waved her glass towards the house. 'I still can't believe you were prepared to sacrifice your lovely home for me.'

'Well, I can't believe you've sacrificed the money you'd set aside for your business just to buy this place.'

'Being crazy is fun, isn't it?' She laughed. 'But thank heavens we've worked as a team. You've heroically offered to finance my business, and I've graciously invited you to stay on living here.'

She reached for his hand. 'But don't forget, Jude, I can sell this place back to you in a blink. It's only a matter of paperwork.' She looked up at him, her blue eyes suddenly serious. 'Perhaps we should sort that out sooner rather than later. I certainly don't want you to risk your capital on my little business.'

'I wouldn't dream of reneging on that promise. You've seen enough small businesses come and go. You know the financial ropes better than I do. I'm sure my money's in safe hands.'

'That's very trusting of you.' Emily drank more bubbles and smiled at him over the rim of her glass. 'So I guess it's official. We're both as crazy as each other.'

'I guess we are.' Setting his glass aside, Jude placed his hands on the timber railing, on either side of her. Trapping her.

Her eyes widened and pretty colour rose in her cheeks. Her lips softened and parted.

'If we're both so crazy,' he said, 'we must be a perfect match.'

'I think we must be.'

They smiled into each other's eyes and it was a smile that reached all the way inside, a smile that made and kept promises.

They'd taken such a roundabout route to be together. They'd both held back, for all kinds of reasons. But now, as Jude kissed Emily, she linked her arms around his neck and their kiss was deep and lush and long, and buoyed by a happy confidence that sent Jude's last barriers tumbling.

He felt so good to be free. No fears. No regrets. No doubts, or what ifs.

Who would have thought total commitment could be so liberating?

'And now,' Emily said, breaking into his thoughts and giving him a cheeky grin, 'I think it's high time you showed me the rest of this house that I've paid an exorbitant amount of money for.'

'So you want a grand tour?'

'Well, there's at least one room I haven't seen.'

'What's that?'

'The master bedroom.'

Jude grinned. 'Which just happens to be the best room in the house.'

Emily totally agreed. The master bedroom was beyond amazing, with an enormous platform bed plus an en suite bathroom with a sunken spa looking out through a wall of glass into a totally private patch of forest. *And* there was even a sliding glass roof.

'For watching the stars at night,' Jude explained.

'Hmm…I think I've made a very sound investment.' She slanted him a questioning smile. 'I hope the master himself is part of this bedroom package?'

'That's a guarantee.' With a sexy growl he pulled her into his arms and set about proving he was as good as his word. Tenderly, but masterfully.

EPILOGUE

THE door to Alex's apartment opened and light spilled onto the steps.

'Jude! Emily!' Alex sent a startled grin to both of them in turn. 'What a surprise.'

'Sorry we didn't warn you we were coming,' said Jude.

'No problem. I'm glad to see you. Come on in.' In the hallway Alex turned back to look at them again. Clearly, he was puzzled. 'What's going on with you two? I know you're an item now, but you both look like you're about to burst.'

'We have good news,' said Emily. 'At least we think it's good news. I'm sure you will, too.'

'Don't tell me Jude's finally finished his book?'

'Actually, yes, I have.' Jude waved a large packet. 'I've even brought you a printout of the manuscript.'

'And I've read it and it's brilliant,' added Emily.

Alex's eyes widened. 'That definitely calls for

a celebration. I wasn't sure he'd ever finish it with you as a distraction, Ems.'

'Well, he's not only finished it, he's started another. And I've also brought wine,' said Emily. 'And cheese and crackers.'

'There's no question then—it's party time.'

Alex hurried ahead of them into the kitchen, grabbing glasses and a plate for the cheese and crackers, as well as olives and pâté from his fridge.

Emily thought how nice it was to be back inside these familiar walls. It was especially nice to have Jude here with her, looking hunky and gorgeous, and with none of that haunting uncertainty in his eyes.

Almost like coming home.

She remembered the meals she and Jude had prepared and shared in this kitchen. The conversations and the revelations. And the tears.

This was where it had all begun and where it had almost ended.

She and Jude had talked about it often. He'd told her how he'd fallen for her on that first night when she'd arrived on his doorstep. And they'd talked about everything that had followed—the morning of the cream nightgown, the kiss where she'd slapped him, the trips to see the heron and the sunset, the fateful striptease…

Jude had been amazingly understanding and patient. He totally *got* how hard it was for her to truly believe and trust that a man could love her as deeply and as permanently as she loved him.

Now, coming back here, Emily realised how wonderfully well Jude's reassurance had worked. She felt truly strong now. Safe and certain. And bone-deep happy.

'Well, well,' said Alex, handing her a glass. 'So what's the news? Apart from the fact that you two are an item.'

'Jude's asked me to marry him,' Emily announced, unable to hold back a moment longer.

Alex's jaw dropped. 'Amazing!'

Jude cuffed his friend on the shoulder. 'You're supposed to say congratulations.'

'I will. I am. I'm saying it now. Congratulations.' Alex's face broke into an enormous grin. 'I didn't know you had it in you, Jude.'

'Granny's not surprised,' countered Emily.

'She's probably been hoping for weeks, the old romantic.'

Just the same, Alex held his arms wide and enveloped Emily in a bear hug. 'Truly, darling, I'm thrilled. You've made an excellent choice.' He shot a wink over his shoulder to Jude. 'So have you, mate.'

'Glad you approve,' Jude responded dryly. 'Just as well you do approve, actually. I was thinking of asking you to be my best man.'

'But then I came up with the brilliant idea that you could be our best person,' Emily broke in. 'Because you're so important to both of us.'

'Oh, goodness. Look at me. I've gone all jammy. If I'm a mess now, how am I going to be on the big day?'

'Perfect,' Emily and Jude said together.

They grinned at each other and Emily felt the happy shiver of desire and the solid kernel of warmth that she felt every time she looked into Jude's eyes. Finally, she'd found happiness—of the lasting kind—for now and for ever.

* * * * *

Mills & Boon® Large Print
September 2012

A VOW OF OBLIGATION
Lynne Graham

DEFYING DRAKON
Carole Mortimer

PLAYING THE GREEK'S GAME
Sharon Kendrick

ONE NIGHT IN PARADISE
Maisey Yates

VALTIERI'S BRIDE
Caroline Anderson

THE NANNY WHO KISSED HER BOSS
Barbara McMahon

FALLING FOR MR MYSTERIOUS
Barbara Hannay

THE LAST WOMAN HE'D EVER DATE
Liz Fielding

HIS MAJESTY'S MISTAKE
Jane Porter

DUTY AND THE BEAST
Trish Morey

THE DARKEST OF SECRETS
Kate Hewitt

0812 Rom LP

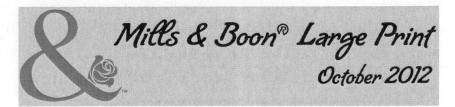

Mills & Boon® Large Print
October 2012

A SECRET DISGRACE
Penny Jordan

THE DARK SIDE OF DESIRE
Julia James

THE FORBIDDEN FERRARA
Sarah Morgan

THE TRUTH BEHIND HIS TOUCH
Cathy Williams

PLAIN JANE IN THE SPOTLIGHT
Lucy Gordon

BATTLE FOR THE SOLDIER'S HEART
Cara Colter

THE NAVY SEAL'S BRIDE
Soraya Lane

MY GREEK ISLAND FLING
Nina Harrington

ENEMIES AT THE ALTAR
Melanie Milburne

IN THE ITALIAN'S SIGHTS
Helen Brooks

IN DEFIANCE OF DUTY
Caitlin Crews

0912 Rom LP